GW00492586

TO KARL

WITH THANKS AND

BEST WISHES

22·3·2021

Return to Segais

By Anthony Murphy

Am he i l-lind
I am salmon in pool

– Amergin Glúngeal

Dedicated to two remarkable humans
who have greatly inspired this work:

C. G. Jung &
John Moriarty

Published by Anthony Murphy, 80 Cedarfield,
Donore Road, Drogheda, Co. Louth, Ireland.
Email: mythicalireland@gmail.com
Website: www.mythicalireland.com

Text copyright © Anthony Murphy
First published 2021
Printed by Anglo Printers Ltd, Drogheda

ISBN 978-1-9993500-1-7

Other books by the author
Non-fiction:
Island of the Setting Sun: In Search of Ireland's Ancient Astronomers
(with Richard Moore), Liffey Press, 2006/2008/2020
Newgrange: Monument to Immortality, Liffey Press, 2012
The Mythology of Venus – Ancient Calendars and Archaeoastronomy
(collaborative, edited by Helen Benigni), University Press of
America, 2013
Mythical Ireland: New Light on the Ancient Past, Liffey Press, 2017
Dronehenge: *The Story Behind the Remarkable Discovery at
Newgrange,* Liffey Press, 2019

Fiction:
Land of the Ever–Living Ones, 2013
The Cry of the Sebac, 2016

CONTENTS

Subscribers

A special word of thanks to the following subscribers who supported the publication of Return to Segais on GoFundMe and PayPal:

Anne McCallum, Mandy McKerl, Marianna Dunn, Marsha Downs, Joan McHugh, Deborah W Johnston, Wandy van der Vlugt, Paul O'Brien, Karl Walsh, Timothy Quinn, Nikki Harte, Jayne Myatt, Shannon Donahue, Caroline Engrand, Judith White, Fiona Nic Giolla Cheara, Fiona Tinker, John Main, Kathleen Freeman, Paul Murphy, Deirdre McSweeney-Kelly, Sandra Defelice-Payne, Paul McNally, Adrienne McArdle, Cyril Carr, Michael and Jeanette Naylor, Sheelagh Gunn, Jenna McGeoghegan, Barbara Barney, Patricia Langton, Barbara Jordan, Sue Prenter, Frederick McKenna, Stephen O Hara, Hazel O'Hanlon, John Huggard, Shawn M Lockhart, Catherine Matheson, Janet Moran, Shereen Dignam, Judith Nilan, Gerard Corcoran, Nicholas Casterton, Indy Riggs, Yvette Tillema, Robin Rickman, Neil Hughes, Domhnall Gillard, Helen Tjader, Cornelia Skipton, Ciara Gleeson, Pat Burns, Shannon Winakur, Miriam Doyle-Baschat, Tim Kavanagh, Niall Flynn, Des Grant, Christine Lange, Tomaí Ó Conghaile, Allen Hubener, Rowen Grove, Kathy Kelly, Cynthia Rogers, Andrew Byrne and Nuala Doyle. Thank you!

Acknowlegements

To my wife Ann and my wonderful children Amy, Luke, Josh, Tara and Finn, I extend my love and gratitude. They are, as ever, incredibly supportive of my writing endeavours and infinitely patient as I immerse myself in many literary pursuits.

I owe a great debt of gratitude to Laura Murphy, who has steadfastly supported my fiction writing over the years. It was Laura's gift of a beautiful hardback notebook that prompted me to begin writing *Return to Segais*. Laura also proofread this book and was immensely supportive during the period of its incubation. I am very grateful also to Treacy O'Connor for first introducing me to the wonders of Uisneach, a truly beautiful, magical and special place.

The wonderful artistic talents of Sean Fitzgerald are to be seen on the cover of this book. Sean was immediately enthusiastic about designing an emblem for the cover that resonated with the book, and I am very grateful to him for his work.

I am indebted to the Mythical Ireland Community, a diverse and wonderful gathering of lovely people from around the world who have enthusiastically followed the work of Mythical Ireland on the internet and various social media sites.

A special word of thanks to Mythical Ireland patrons at www.patreon.com/mythicalireland. Their generous patronage has helped bring this literary endeavour to fruition.

Thanks to Fiona Nic Giolla Cheara, Marie Lendon, Vanessa Morgan, Donna Firer, Jo Butler, Lee Williams, Mandy McKerl, Marlin Ó Ciarmhaic, Joan McHugh, Stephen O Hara and Timothy E. Quinn for their magnanimous assistance.

I am also grateful to my parents and siblings and a wider circle of relatives and friends who have been hugely supportive over the years. I am hoping that you find your faithful support justified by my meagre literary efforts!

FOREWORD

This is not a conventional book. It emerged from some unknown wellspring of myth and poetry, something that, like Segais itself, was brimming with energy, on the verge of a fluid emergence, a fountain of words. These words were written, carefully and lovingly with a pen, onto the creamy pages of a beautiful notebook. Before I began, I set clear intentions and proscriptions – that the writing would not follow any plan or formula, that the resulting book should not be defined easily as a text of fiction or non-fiction, that I would not count its words, and that it would be allowed to flow freely onto those creamy pages. What followed was a most extraordinary emanation.

Return to Segais is a story of human experience and an exploration of the depths of the human unconscious through mythology, exemplified by the life cycle of the salmon, a singularly remarkable creature which is able to survive in fresh water as well as salt water. Having been spawned in the breeding pools of the upper reaches of the river Boyne, represented in myth by the symbolic Well of Segais, the salmon eventually finds its way to the sea, and the ocean, before ultimately returning to the exact location of its birth, where, in its final act, it spawns the next generation of salmon.

Within the wonderfully diverse myths of the river Boyne, including those about the famed Salmon of

Knowledge, the story of the arrival of the Milesian bard Amergin and the myths of the great monuments of Brú na Bóinne, are powerful metaphors and poetic signposts for the ordinary mortal human who might dare to wish to live an exemplary mythical existence.

Joseph Campbell, in *The Hero With a Thousand Faces*, wrote that: 'Myth is the secret opening through which the inexhaustible energies of the cosmos pour into human cultural manifestation'.

Return to Segais attempts to serve as a means of allowing the invigorating, revivifying and life-affirming waters of the sacred well to pour into the human experience, with all its lows and highs, all its struggles and successes, all its tragedies and its triumphs, and to express by mythic and poetic means those experiences of the otherworld that, in Ireland, is eternally on the cusp of a great overflowing into this world.

There is something about myth that is at once familiar, and yet wholly ineffable. At times, it makes perfect sense, and at others is entirely impenetrable.

Some time ago, perhaps many years ago, I realised the futility of attempting to transcribe or otherwise adapt or decipher in their entirety the images and metaphors of the myths of the Boyne Valley. It was easier, I found, to frame stories and narratives around the symbolism of myth, rather than to endeavour to provide some sort of rational or explicit explanation of their complete meaning.

The mythology of Ireland is a bit like the megalithic art inscribed upon the kerb stones of the great *sídhe* mounds of the Neolithic. Some of that art seems entirely translatable, but some is opaque and apparently incomprehensible.

Many of the tens of thousands of visitors who come to Síd in Broga (Newgrange) every year ask what is the meaning of the triple spiral emblem carved onto the great kerb stone that lies at its entrance.

The real question is this – does the triple spiral have an explicit meaning? Was it ever intended to have a pedagogical, instructive function? Or, in its flagrant abstraction, was it supposed to lead the initiate on labyrinthine journeys into the depths of their own human fallibility and unconscious infinitude?

Like the megalithic art, some myths are pliable in the hands of the writer, explainable in rational terms. Others are intransigent, refusing to yield to logical stimulus or interpretation.

And so, sometimes all that is left for us to do is to retell the story and allow it to do its own talking.

There are facets of the journey that are much easier to navigate, belonging as they do to the everyday experience of the human being.

But there are aspects of this story that are, by necessity, couched in vague and arcane allegory and abstract themes. How can I explain to you that which is unfathomable? I am unable, being just an ordinary human being. Words are inadequate.

In this respect, I recall the poet, evoking Amergin, the mythical bard whose birth of song is as much a disclosure of the universal desire for illumination as it is a revelation of his own personal gnosis. In his incantation are flashes of poetic brilliance that call us to deeper, hidden aspects of ourselves.

The journey of the salmon seems an apt metaphor for the experience of human life. The injunction at Segais, before the smolt leaves the 'nest', so to speak, is to go forth and find the ocean, and in finding the ocean, to find something of itself that is unattainable except in rare circumstances.

A prolonged meditation upon the wonderfully rich and diverse mythic images presented in the Irish storytelling tradition yields glimpses into that deep unknown, unknowable depth of human consciousness and unconsciousness.

In *Return to Segais,* I summon Bradán Feasa, the Salmon of Knowledge, and Amergin, and Bóinn, and Dagda, and Manannán, and Oengus, and Ériu, and a host of others from the mythological pantheon, to take us to those depths, and perhaps beyond.

The truth is that there is no vastness greater than the deep and yawning chasm of our own innocence, our own unknowing. But it is surely a great joy to attempt to explore that vast boundlessness of the human spirit.

Anthony Murphy
Drogheda
January 2021

A River of Ink

The pen rests 2mm from the paper. All the will in the world will not push it down. The gods themselves could heave down upon it and it would not budge. It is suspended, resting between its wielder's finger and thumb, waiting … waiting.

Even the greatest forces cannot make the pen do what the sword does willingly. A tiny figure dances on the pen's lid, placed over its far end.

'Down, down, push it down,' the figure shouts in a tiny voice, dancing and stamping and prancing upon it, willing it to move like a tiny ant trying to force the earth out of its orbit. Here now is the writer's bane — the 'block' that holds back all the forces of the universe.

'Don't push here,' the warning sign reads.

Another exclaims: 'Warning. Words ahead!'

The pen moves, and worlds quake in darkness. The scribe has awoken. Deep thoughts stir. The blood pulses through the fingers. Here, in the lamplight of a desolate evening, words are being born.

'Press down now,' urges a gentle voice. 'Do it!'

But the pen declines.

'Where do I start?' someone asks.

'Start at the beginning, of course,' comes the reply, from the same source.

'But I do not know where that is.'

'You will find out.'

The beginning. A moment ordained. A moment preordained. Find a nice pen. One that you are comfortable writing with. And a nice notebook. A notebook etched with the words of one who was excitedly imbued with the flowing river of word's thoughts. Follow that river. Where is its source? Where should I hook my berry to my hazel wand? Into what waters should I let it plunge? What words will it pull out of the belly of that smolt?

'See now, you have written a page!'

Its creamy paper is decorated with black characters. The notebook has become a stage — a stage for dreams, and words, and a winding river.

'What river?'

A river of thoughts that winds backwards through the landscapes of our better nature. That nature that first urged us to sound, and song, and speech, and words. Here, in this moment, eternity meets me in the nib of a pen, with its mighty river of ink that drowns my every thought in permanence. If this notebook should last a hundred years (and I doubt it), where will I be when you read its words, a century from now? When is now?

INBER COLPA

I saw a salmon in the stream. It shimmered and gleamed, a vision in the darkness. A fish that swam through a river of black ink to the spawning pools of my imagination. And the water gushes down, black like oil, from the darkest fountain of my first form. Before I was me, I was me. Before I was me, I was something. My first form – the spawn of what I was to become – lay there in a shallow pool of blackness, hidden from time.

'You are not yet to be.'

Like the word that was yet to be born of darkly letters on a creamy page, you hung there, like the pen nib, suspended in air, suspended in ink, suspended in the black pool, awaiting that call, that birth of song.

That birth of song — your *amher-ghin* — could not be willed by god, nor beast, nor the urgings of fate. Your *amher-ghin* would come when the glimmering salmon had made its way, with luck as a companion, through the murky river of black ink to the spawning pools of your first utterings.

'Mother. My Father.' They don't sound the same.

'*Máthair. M'Athair.*' They do sound the same.

Máthair. M'Athair. What was born there in the murky pool? What was conceived there in the first brimming of the well of Segais? When the first trickle of water tumbled over its edge, what had Bóinn done that led to the breaking of her soul?

In the first morning of our being, when the waters break and we rush away from Segais, what do we bring with us that will prevent the breaking of our soul?

What miracle should be wrought there, at Segais, so that we may venture from soul to sea, from well to ocean, from spawning ground to heaven's gate, and remain incorruptible?

Where have we been, the moon and I, since we left Segais on that morning when the waters broke?

The white cow, she who gleams and ungleams. *Mo Mháthair.* My Mother. My water. Since you brought me down, I've been trying to get back to the spawning pools of my first utterings. I should say that I am sorry. In my journeys back to the spawning pools of my imagination, swimming with the salmon, and the trout, and the eel, I have broken many a limb while jumping the weirs of our impossibilities. And as I swam, from Inber Colpa to the well of Segais, the water turned from silvery blue to murky brown to the darkest black. And I lost my way to the place where time and reason announce themselves to an eternal soul. In the blackest nights I travelled, without starlight or moonlight, seeking that bright, wandering cow, that bright, wandering salmon. But they put me wayward on the Milky Way. A wayward soul, lost on the great journey from womb to tomb. My star, lost amid many.

Beset and besieged by the otter at the weir, and the heron on the bank, I left the river, and opted instead to find my way across land. Out of water, in the bright light of day, I would reach those spawning pools, and find the source, that which had ordained me in the deep and shining waters of Segais.

By chance, I found myself an Inber Colpa, on Bealtaine eve, at the water's edge, with Bóinn lapping at my feet. I saw a dog, walking along the river bank. He stopped and looked at me, the wanderer lost.

The dog spoke.

'This is as far as I go,' he said. 'To go any further would just put salt in the wounds.'

Salt in the wounds. Salt and stinging. A harsh treatment for the wounds of the lost pilgrim, who is stinging already from the bitter abrasions of the pilgrimage.

Inber Colpa. The meeting of the waters. The place where fresh water and salt water meet. To go any further would risk salt in the wounds. The shin bone of the monster washed down to here. It could go no further because of the salt in the wound. The monster, Mata. Mata, *mo mháthair*. The mother of all beasts. Torn limb from limb at Brú na Bóinne, it was thrown into the water. Perhaps it, too, had become waylaid on the journey to the spawning grounds of our imagination.

Its giant frame, sundered by our devious nature, would endure in the silvery waters, a constant reminder to us of our own monster nature.

The monster that was broken on the Lecc Benn could not be broken again, only cured by the salt water. The Mata got a kick in the shin at Inber Colpa. A stinging wound.

But how did Bóinn fare out, at the meeting of the ancient waters? The salt in her wounds was too much. Deprived of an eye, and a hand, and a leg, the goddess was blemished. In her blemished condition, she passed here, rushing out to sea for the salting of her wounds. There was nothing in her blemished nature that could be washed clean with the salt of the sea. But maybe there was nothing blemished in her nature at all.

The bright cow of many parts, she who is illuminated, came to Inber Colpa from Segais well, but there was nothing so sullied in her nature that she couldn't shine again. The ingress of salt into the wound was caused by a transgression, a trespass, into the sensibilities of the male caste. But the wandering cow will be renewed again when the salt in the wounds becomes the glue that holds her together.

Bóinn/Eithne/mother/*máthair*/Mata, meet cruelty with compassion, and be the salt water that washes the wounded clean. Bear their pain upon your wounded back down to Inber Colpa and out to sea. There, we might chance upon your little lapdog by the shore, and he will guard the meeting of the waters to watch what passes in the night.

First came the ice. And then the water. Then the fish, followed by the other creatures. And after a while, the boats came. And the men and women. Inber Colpa, you have seen much since our form was first founded in the wakening of the world. There were many dreary days before the first bird song was heard along the banks of the Boyne. But the birth of song was a symphony of joy, when the ears of the land itself opened to the sound of creation's better nature. Should we dare to ask, or even contemplate, where the bird song was created?

That was a good day, when the dreariness of the ages was first punctuated by the sound of birdsong. Men and women need never feel alone when they can hear the sound of a bird. And I wonder, what bird was it that was first heard at Inber Colpa. Which bird had the great honour of calling out across the waters of the Boyne, to hear the echo of its own incantation from the woods along its edge?

Was it the curlew or the swan? The gull or the gannet? The song thrush or the blackbird? The robin or the goldfinch?

When the first drops of water trickled down from the hill above Sídh Nechtain, and Bóinn was born of a million rain showers, what call would change that water to golden honey at the meeting of the waters?

What water droplet could not be impelled to rush towards Inber Colpa so that its very form would be transformed by the vibrations of a melody emanating from the heavens?

Bóinn herself could be remade by the call of the curlew at the estuary of the Boyne, where fresh water meets salt water; where the silence of eternity is broken by the voice from the air. There is no wound that could not be healed by the sound of a slender-beaked curlew. Even Dian Cécht himself would bow in obeisance to the birds, those whose sound can call down heaven and bring the gods to heel.

When you hear the call of the curlew by the Boyne in the evening, you will surely live forever. And as the robin and blackbird sing out the last light of day, your soul will be greatly heartened in the safe knowledge that the night is just a passing thing, and tomorrow the light will come again. The salt water and the fresh water lap in joy at the river's edge to the sound of the curlew at Inber Colpa.

Isn't the salmon a remarkable creature, that it can abide in waters fresh and salty? The salmon passes effortlessly from fresh water to salt water at Inber Colpa. Some salmon make return journeys. Passing up and down the Boyne, from sea to spawning pools and back again, the salmon nods to Bóinn's lapdog by the shore.

Bóinn was broken here.

Mata was broken here.

But the salmon swims on, impervious to the dismemberment of flesh; oblivious to the dismemberment of soul; insouciant about the dismemberment that tears sinew from bone in the undoing of our untrumpeted virtues.

Inber Colpa, the meeting of the waters.
Inber Colpa, the parting of the waters.
Inber Colpa, the parting of the ways.

The salmon swims, untroubled, into the great open sea. But the remnants of the goddess, and the remnants of the monster, are there to remind him that the passage from source to sea, from the spawning pools of our first utterings to the open ocean of our imaginations, is not an easy way from a state of innocence to a state of bliss. Many have come undone on the journey from source to serenity.

The waters trickle down from Segais, and cascade down from Segais, and gush down from Segais. At first, the journey seems an effortless one. A peaceful one. But there are many obstacles and many traps and many shaded pools on the journey down from Segais to Inber Colpa and onwards to the great ocean. In every journey from source to sea and back again, the salmon is beset with and besieged by the snags and snares that would prove the undoing of a lesser, or even a greater, god.

Watch now, for the otter at the weir.

Watch now, for the angler's hook.

Watch now, for the heron by the shore.

Many of our dismembered parts lie scattered upon the river bed, and by the shore of the sparkling Boyne. The remnants of our wounded ego are there, in the eddying pools where the great river meanders between apathy and insouciance. The arm and leg of Bóinn are there, broken by the rushing waves, broken before reaching the ocean. The bones of the Mata are there, gleaming in the pool, a shimmering sign that all may not run with ease on that great rush from Segais to sea.

And in the winter of our broken spirit, we see scattered on the banks by the weir the bones of many a salmon who came undone in the great leap out of water.

Those bones, those bones. Those scattered bones.

A remarkable fish, the salmon. It can abide in fresh water. It can abide in salt water. In can even abide, for short moments, in the air.

A fish out of water.

A fish that can fly.

Fly me a river, thou magical salmon.

Take to the air, marvellous creature of the ocean, and the sea, and the river, and the well, and the shallow pool. But be careful. Make sure you look before you leap. That's what a salmon does, before it jumps a weir.

I stood at the shore of the Boyne at Inber Colpa on a spring evening with the water lapping at my feet. It was low tide. In the twilight, the first crescent moon and the Evening Star were paired in the low western sky, a duo of old friends meeting once again on their eternal round.

As I stood there, on the rocks at low tide, with the water touching my feet, I wondered if it wasn't calling me to a deeper life, a life imbued with many journeys of the heart, from shallow pools to deep ocean. Was it akin to a gentle tap on the shoulder, this incessant lapping at my feet? A calling, perhaps, to the life of a fish?

Just like the salmon at the weir is a fish out of water, I wondered if perhaps I should become a man out of air. Or out of earth.

BÓINN REMADE

There is a strange calling, an indescribable beckoning, that comes to you on the shore of the sea. It is a calling to a bigger life. A life beyond what you can imagine or comprehend. The life of a sailor, maybe, but not a crewman on a merchant ship, but rather the oarsman of an ancient coracle, a boat covered with the hide of a cow, an ocean-sweeper bobbing up and down, relentlessly searching the oceans of your eternal dreams for that flickering, silvery light in the rivers and seas of your darkest depths.

Should I wade out now, I wondered, into the Boyne at Mornington, in search of that silvery sliver of light in the vast darkness? And in doing so, would I become Manannán, keeper of the sea, lord of the oceans? The Manannán of Mornington, the one who plunges into the pool of our innocent dawn and emerges from the western ocean at the last light of evening, with a fish in his hand.

What have you seen there, in the murky depths of the seas of our unknowing, O great lord of the oceans?

Did the salmon pass you by in the night? A flicker of light.

Did Bóinn pass you by? Broken Bóinn, the fragments of her impetuousness shimmering in the shallows.

Did the Mata pass you by in the night? The frame of the beast. The shank of the beast. The ribcage of the beast, a monstrous thing to be set down in the shallow ford of our dark pool, our *dubh linn*?

And if all three passed you by, which one would you follow? Would you chase the gleaming fish, on its journey from darkness to light, from sea to soul? Knowing that the salmon is searching for the spawning grounds of your first thoughts, would you follow instead the body of Bóinn, broken Bóinn, wounded Bóinn, to the craggy shores of Rockabill?

O mother Bóinn, when the waters first broke, you brought me into the world. But now the waters have broken you. Alas that it should be so. Mother, you are the river, with the lapdog by the shore. How do we remake you?

And I wonder — if I should go down to the shore of the sea at Inber Colpa in the morning, would I chance upon Bóinn remade, emerging from the water of her reglorification, the water of her deep immersion? If the Boyne could break her, maybe the sea could remake her? Having run her course from source to sea, she might now desire to, salmon-like, return to the spawning pools of her first imaginations.

What if Bóinn should go back to Segais? What power would Segais and its taboos have over the remade goddess of our midnight dreams? In these dreams from the witching hour, we have seen the broken goddess float out to sea; in one dream, her broken pieces form islands in the sea. She is creation. Creation in destruction. In another dream, we see her float down from Segais, past Inber Colpa, and in the light of the bright full moon, we see Bóinn remade in the lunar pool — the pool of the bright moon, the pool of the illuminated cow.

The broken moon, shattered by its daytime encounter with the scorching sun, is remade in the evening when it rises whole out of the sea in opposition to a setting sun. In her everlasting journey around Segais, Bóinn is broken and rebroken. The wounded moon rises later each night, with larger and greater chunks removed from its face of cow-hide. Eventually, all that's left is a slender crescent in the morning twilight — the horns of the dying and broken cow.

And then she disappears.

For three days, she is gone.

In myth, the cow and the calf become islands. They are dead, but undead.

Shall we, the hopeless few, wait by the shore of her undoing for a resurrection? Or should we follow Manannán way out west, to the great ocean, to watch for the renewed cow horns of her miraculous return, the defaced Bóinn who is being refaced after her scourging by the sun?

Come back to us now, at the turning of the tide. Bring the tide to our feet by the shore, us hopeless few, grey-faced pilgrims, bereft at the breaking of the illuminated cow.

Before the dawn, you disappeared, swallowed by the rising waters of Segais. We, the ashen-faced pilgrims on the way of the white cow, found that the path beneath our feet had vanished, replaced by a river of black oil that swamped our darkened toes. And we lost our way, because the bright woman of our midnight dreams had been broken by a fiery dawn that would burn our dreams to a blackened charcoal. And what should we do with the blackened coals of our burnt-out dreams? What should we do with the charcoal, by the shore in the morning of our undoing?

Should we alchemists feed the charcoal of your ruination to the magic heron by the shore, in the hope that it lays a silver egg, glistening in the morning of our hopeless resolutions?

And if I should happen upon that silver egg in the morning of my misgivings, would I mistake it for Manannán's treasure bag — full of promise at high tide, but devoid of hope when the sea draws out its treasure with the detritus in the evening of the ebbing tide?

I've had many misgivings about writing this book. Should I now tear it asunder, like broken Bóinn, and scatter its meaning-laden, meaningless fragments upon the heaving waters? The notebook is a treasure bag of thoughts. Pregnant with possibility in the morning of our blank pages, it becomes filled with the words and thoughts and distracted musings of our distracted lives. The words build up behind the pen. The nib is the pressure point of our poetic power. It is the bottleneck where the traffic snarls up; the shower cloud laden with a downpour.

When enough pressure rises behind the nib, the pen bursts into life, and the words emerge, just like the treasure bag is revealed by the retreating tide.

But in the drawing back of the tide, what if we should see the bones of Bóinn, or the bones of the Mata, strewn on the shore? What treasure bag would that be to our eyes?

I would wince at the sight, but might marvel at the wonder of Manannán's treasure bag, and its renewal by the tide. What if Bóinn could be remade, in silvery raiment, her unbroken form glimmering in the morning half-light?

What then could Éire become?

Oh mother, come to me, in the half-light. Your wandering son, weary of the daily treading of dangerous paths. Call me Oengus Óg, the one who is born on the evening of the day of his conception, and I shall take you by the hand, and lead you to the altar of reconstitution, the holy pit of rebirth.

And then, perhaps, the only invasion upon our chaste shores will be by the pages of a book of taking — the leaves of vellum, etched with the words of the scribe's desire, strewn on the strand like the forlorn fragments of the Mata's body. On the altar of your revival, the sacred plinth of your rejuvenation, the treasure of all of

Manannán's lofty days will be brought and laid before the great queen of the morning.

Bóinn, we shall see you remade, so that the dark days will be banished, and so that only the light of the dawn of your recreation will be seen to shine in the dim corners of our neglect.

I looked at you once, and saw deep down a sky full of stars, and a world that was new, and a heart that knew gladness. In the quickening twilight, I caught a glimpse of something, down there in the depths of blue. It was a flickering light, a light from the old world. I imagined I was seeing something from an antediluvian earth, a glimpse into a world of aeons past, long before the first virgin footsteps on the shore of this sacred island. And as I looked deep into the water, the image flashed and flickered and glimmered, so that I was hopelessly unsure of what I saw.

'The old world is still in you, boy,' a voice said.

'You have come a long way since your first emergence from the birth waters.'

As the voice spoke, I saw a flash, and a face briefly appeared. And, like the voice, I could not tell whether the face was that of a woman or a man.

'I am Manannán,' it said.

'I am Ériu,' it said.

'I am Fintan.'

'I am Bóinn.'

'I am Amergin.'

'I am Mata.'

'I am you.'

And, as it said that, I saw a white swan gliding past, flying in a sky beneath those waters. Then I saw a salmon, jumping into the air with a dance of de-lice, a dance of delight. Then I saw a silver egg. It cracked open, and a pig appeared. The pig turned into a dog, and then a man, and after a short while the man grew wings and became a hawk. And when he took flight, the waters shimmered and glistened, but as they calmed, there was a great bone, a shin bone or a thigh bone, down there in the water.

'I am the Mata, the monster of the old world,' a great voice said.

'I am the Mata, the maker of the new world.'

As the voice said that, the water glimmered again and there was something bright, shining from the depths. It was a pale light, silvery and blue at first but warming as it got brighter. It grew in size and intensity until it was so bright it was like the sun at noon, and I found it hard to look at. There was something moving in the light. Or someone. The vivid golden orange glow was like a brilliant, radiant sun, down there in the reflected sky of another world. A shadow moved about in the light. I could see the outline of a boy. He was a young boy, no more than about nine or ten years of age. He was in a tunnel, immersed in the brilliant light. Shortly, I could see a glint of metal, a shiny blade. There was a sword, embedded deep in a rock wall.

'Who are you?' a voice called out from the darkness.

The boy peered into the void, but said nothing. He turned towards the sword. As he did so, I saw giant hands coming down either side of him, touching at the fingertips, as if in prayer. The hands formed a tunnel, bathed in golden light.

'Who are you?' the great voice boomed out again.

The boy turned his gaze back into the gloom.

'Would it matter, whether I said I was the boy Sétanta, lost on his way across Muirthemne plain, or Dagda, entering the house of Elcmar?'

'It matters greatly,' said the voice. 'For who shall rouse the sleeping army — a mere boy, or the great god himself?'

And in the darkness, there was a great stirring.

THE LAVA-LIGHT

As the boy turned towards the sword in the wall, the scene shimmered and darkened and I was whisked away, as if being pulled into some maelstrom of spiralling energy, down, down into the deep waters, towards the bottom of the ocean. In the depths, there was a hole in the bed of the sea. It was strange — a square hole, cut into the rock. Light like lava flowed out, emanating like heat from some unknown source.

'You have to go in there.'

That was the instruction, which resounded from somewhere in my own mind. I couldn't imagine even trying. It was a small hole, and the heat and light streamed out in yellow and orange and red tendrils, as if all the energy of another world was seeping out through this mysterious aperture. As I stared, in trepidation and wonder, I saw shapes and patterns before my eyes. There were parallel lines and diamonds and circles; bright and dim undulating patterns. And then a bright light appeared in front of me. A white-blue brilliant light. It felt safe to go towards the light, so I did.

Shortly, I found myself lying on my back looking up into a blue sky. I could hear water, and there was sand beneath my hands. I sat up abruptly. I was lying on the shore of a river, not far from where it would enter the sea. The river banks to my left were shrouded above the beach line in a great canopy of green.

CALMING THE STORM

A man came walking up the beach. He had a purposeful stride. He looked, as the saying goes, like a man on a mission.

'Where are you going?' I asked him.

He turned to look at me, seeming surprised by my presence.

'I am going,' he said, with a voice full of authority, 'to invoke the land of Ireland.'

I got up from where I had been sitting.

'How does one invoke the land of Ireland?' I asked, full of curiosity.

'In the same way that one calms the storm,' he replied. 'Did you see the storm?'

'Oh, I have seen many a storm,' I said, fearlessly.

He looked surprised. Impatient almost. He pointed out towards the sea and said: 'Do you see how the water is now calm? Just an hour ago it was tossing my boat about like a trinket in a bathtub. I was sure I was done for.'

The truth is that I hadn't noticed the storm. Not because it hadn't happened, but because I was deep down in the waters, looking at the square hole cut into the seabed. The hole out of which the lava-light flowed.

'You have to go in there,' said a voice in my mind. Perhaps it would have been as easy for me to enter the lava-light hole as it was for the stranger to have landed

21

at the estuary in a storm. To be honest, it seemed to me that the storm could come at any moment, as it had done, many times. Casting a glance out west, like a fisherman casting a hopeful net into cold ocean waters, I imagined that I could catch a storm with that glance, and bring it ashore to the beach of my own undoing.

I knew that the storm could come in a moment, and could last for years. The only question was whether the storm would beat me, or whether I would outlive its anger and its fierce lashings by swimming down to the lava-light, the golden glow at the sea's bottom, where no storm seemed to dwell.

Many storms came and went. How did I outlive them? Did I stand, warrior-like, on the rocky pinnacle, as if made of rock myself, and bear the burden of its howling winds and torrents of rain? Did I take the lashings, like an old weathered rock on the shore, facing the tempest? Was I petrified? A petrified man, made of stone? Or was I petrified — cowering in fear?

Many times the storm came. Sometimes, I pulled the bed clothes up over my head and trembled, petrified in the darkness. A different kind of petrified.

Worn by the succession of storms, rock slowly becomes sand. If you threw a rock at someone, you would do them a fierce injury. But what if you threw sand? Broken down into tiny grains, the rock loses its strength and power. How might the storm also be thus dissolved?

Instead of bearing the storm as the petrified man on the rock-face, or the petrified man beneath the bed blankets, should I rather be thinking of how to calm the storm? The man on the shore with the purposeful stride would tell me, surely. But I looked around and he was gone.

There was something in what he told me, in our all-too-brief dialogue, that he knew, as much as he knew how to tie his shoelaces, as much as he knew how to put the coat on his back, that he could understand the language of a barking dog, or read the thoughts of a fish. And best of all, he knew, perhaps, how to calm the storm. But he was gone on his mission, to invoke the land of Ireland, and such a mighty and noble mission it seemed to be. No wonder he walked with such a resolute stride!

And as I sat back down on the sandy shore again, to think about it all, and to contemplate the calming of the storm, I sat this time with my back to the sea, so that I was facing westwards, inland. I sat with my back to the sea knowing that even its sound would pull me down to that deeper life, if I allowed it. As I looked, the clouds in the west drew back, and the sun's rays swept over the land, in an act of invocation, perhaps, an illuminating invocation, and the dark strips of cloud parted, like a great mouth opening, as if something remarkable was about to be uttered to the ground, from the sky.

Light had a voice, AEons ago. It spoke. Perhaps, if I could find that opening in the seabed, where the lava-light spewed out, I might hear the voice of the light. It might tell me how to calm the storm.

THE SONG OF AMERGIN

But now, as I looked, the sun became brilliant, and it shone with an intensity so great that I could not look directly at it.

Somewhere in the world, a storm was brewing, perhaps from a lake or pool where the heat of the day was causing an evaporation of water, a calling forth of spawn to a greater life, its steam slowly rising to form the beginning of a thundercloud. But here, on the shore of the river estuary, summer had suddenly broken through the clouds and there was a glorious light.

Buddha-like, I sat, with my hands on my knees, my gaze to the west and my tail-bone stuck in the warm sand. I thought of the words of the sea warrior who had passed by a short time before.

'I invoke the land of Ireland.'

I looked towards the sun and noticed it had dimmed somewhat. But there was no cloud obscuring it. Rather, there was a 'bite' missing from it.

An eclipse!

Soon, the sky was darkening, and shade drew across the land and the water, like a river-drinking monster drawing in slowly. The invisible moon was moving swiftly across the sun, making itself visible by its act of covering. The invisible was becoming visible. Brilliant day was turning quickly to shaded night. The birds fell silent, and the water stilled, as if calmed by some magical work. In a moment, the sun was eclipsed. A brilliant ring of light appeared, with a dark centre. The stars emerged in the quickening twilight. There, beneath the sun, were the brilliant stars of Orion.

The warrior of the light was holding the brilliant shining ring, an engagement ring perhaps, signifying the marriage of the sun and moon, or perhaps even the matrimony between darkness and the light.

As I watched the giant hero, with the halo-light of brilliance high over his head, I imagined that somewhere in the vast universe an old world was coming to an end, like a rock turning to sand, and a new world was just beginning, like a perfect sphere of rock emerging from the grains of a crumbled and vanished and withered creation. The sand of the old world was swept up by the dying waves of a storm and carried down into the half-light of the deep, into the arms of Manannán. The great sphere was lifted up by a giant god and borne with great strength high above his head, to a lofty place in the universe, where a great shimmering light pulsated from it, as if it were a solid star about to ignite at the beginning of its life.

'I will throw it,' the god said, his voice booming so that the ground trembled.

'I will throw it, so that it will find its path, a steady course, a never-ending circle through the sky.'

And he threw the giant globe, and his throw was good. A mighty, long cast, with his Herculean arm. And it seemed to me, sitting on the sandy shore of a world yet young, and still old, that in the far reaches of the cosmos there was life, rejoicing at the birth of the new world from rings of light. To my right, the still water of the river estuary was reflecting perfectly the stars above, so that it seemed that the sky was down there, and not above.

As I stared at this underwater universe, a silvery light streaked past. I could not see what it was, but I imagined that it was a salmon whose name I knew, its silvery back reflecting the light from all the stars in the newly-dimmed sky, and that it was, somehow, racing towards the setting place of Orion, to a spawning pool in the far reaches of the river's birthplace, where the light of the Orion Nebula would be reflected gloriously.

'May Lugh shine a light for you,' I found myself saying aloud.

'For Lugh is a light upon every road and journey.'

And as I said it, the sun's brilliant light spilled out again from behind the moon, and the darkness of night quickly gave way to a pale dawn. In a moment, Orion vanished. All the stars were gone to sleep. But the world was waking, waking to a new birth.

Ireland had been invoked.

And Ireland invoked is Ireland awake, and very much alive. Deep down, in her hollow hills and hidden quarters, there was a great stretching and yawning, an awakening of something that had been slumbering for thousands of years in the body of Ériu. She was pregnant. Pregnant with possibility.

From the setting to the rising of the sun — i.e. in the night of our hero dreaming, our druid dreaming, our Amergin dreaming, our Finn dreaming, our Lugh dreaming — there is no better land. Ireland at night, when Ériu is ensconced in her dreamscape, is a place where possibility marries with magic. In the darkness, a wonder-child is born — the child of the golden sun, and the silver moon; a child of the silver branch and the speckled cow; a child of the speckled salmon and the blood-red nuts of the forest.

The *cnó*-child.

The *bó*-child.

The *bradán*-child stirs in the shadows of the spawning pools of possibility.

Untainted by reason; untainted by rationale; untainted by the mechanics of his emergence, he reaches towards the light. Deep down in the darkness, in the amniotic fluid of the great mother from whom every good thing emerges, the wonder-child strives towards the faint light. Without knowing, he knows. Without feeling, he feels. Without experience, he experiences. In the amniotic fluid of possibility, without dreaming, he dreams. He sees light, and the light is good. Engulfed in potential, the young being — the fledgling, the zygote — has already seen his path before him, even before he knew thought. His path leads out of hell, up to the

light. Long is the road, and hard. But not all roads are paved with gold. At least this one is paved with light.

For now, the salmon spawn rests in the dark pool, the *Dubh Linn,* in the upper reaches of the great river. There will be a glorious birth, because Ériu has been invoked. There will be a glorious birth because she has heard that song again.

What song?

The song of Amergin.

'I am a salmon in a pool. I am a lake on a plain. I am a boar for valour.'

Thank you Amergin, whose name means 'birth of song'. Your song has stirred my heart. The birth of song is a birth of hope — the conception of possibility.

And in all the years I've known you, I've wondered about you. I've doubted you. I've rejected you. I cast you aside, as an interloper. But I was wrong about you. Your birth of song was not a death knell for the Dé Dananns. Rather, it was the sound of a sweet bell, ringing for the sacred marriage of doubt and possibility. For to have doubt is to imagine, in equal measure, both disaster and delight. Doubt is what we experience when we plunge into the deep ocean and, after swimming down and down and down, we encounter only bleak darkness. Does that mean there is no light down there? Does our own darkness quench the light? And if we see that lava-light emanating from the seabed, will our own doubt extinguish it? Or, in seeing the light in our own deepest darkness, will we experience our own birth of song?

Down there, will doubt and possibility intertwine, so that we can grasp that lava-light and bring it to the surface? And if we bring that lava-light to the surface, will it then be possible that Bóinn can be remade?

Ériu thinks it possible.

Banba thinks it possible.

Fodla thinks it possible.

Doubt is the spawning pool of possibility. If you feed doubt with the *cnó* and the salmon flesh and the bones of Mata, and make an invocation, a call for emergence, you might well experience your own birth of song.

THE SALMON AND THE CNÓ

When song is born, many other things are born too. The birth of song is a heavenly realisation. When song is born, nations are born. When song is born, peoples find their communal voice. When song is born, we achieve great things.

In our own pool of doubt, a miracle is wrought. Out of the slime, the smolt emerges. When the lava-light is brought to the surface, a billion possibilities manifest.

'None shall look to the bottom of the well.'

Why? Why is there nobody who will look to the bottom of the well? What is the prohibition that prevents us from doing so?

The reason that it is said no one shall look to the bottom of the well is because in doing so, in bringing our own doubt to Segais, we fear that we will see nothing but darkness in its deepest depths. And then it will erupt upon us, and break us, and wash us down, sweeping like a great river rushing to the sea, and we will drown in the waters of our own doubt.

Only those who have heard the song of Amergin should look to the bottom.

Only those who have seen the shimmering silver light at Inber Colpa should look to the bottom.

Only those who have stood at the sea shore awaiting Bóinn's remaking should look to the bottom.

Bring your doubt to Segais and have it wash over you.

Segais is not a pool of darkness. It is a pool of possibility.

What did the salmon imbibe there, as fry, as smolt, in the depths of Segais?

What was it digesting, when it ate the sacred hazel nuts?

They were the *cnó* of its doubts.

They were the *cnó* of its faults.

They were the *cnó* of its misgivings.

They were the *cnó* of its prejudices.

They were the *cnó* of its self-loathing.

They were the *cnó* of its pride.

They were the *cnó* of its fears.

They were the *cnó* of its fall.

They were the *cnó* of all the things it wanted to know. The *cnó* of knowing. The *cnó* of no return.

Like the apple from the tree of the knowledge of good and evil, to taste the *cnó* of the sacred trees that grew over Segais was to cross a salmon weir from which there could be no return.

The pool of introspection becomes a pool of excoriation. Once the sacred nut is cracked open, it loses its shell. And there is nothing then to prevent its inner core — its true nature — from being revealed. When the salmon ate the *cnó* in Segais, something of its own shell was parted, and something of its skin was

rent open, and something of its own core nature was revealed to itself.

By ingesting the nuts, and consuming their inner seed, the fish was imbibing its own rebirth. The seed was planted in the belly of a fish. The *cnó* of no return had been cracked open, like a fissure opening in the heart of the fish, allowing its past lives to seep out and become manifest.

This was no ordinary salmon. This was Bradán Feasa, the Salmon of Knowledge — the knowledge of good and evil, of present lives and past iterations, of glimpses into the core nature of all living things. A *sídhe* had opened in the heart of the fish, in its very fabric and nature, allowing other worlds to become visible in the pristine waters of the well of Segais.

Faced with such a terrible beauty, the salmon found itself confined by the constraints of the well. Even though the well was thought to have no bottom, the fish whose heart had been opened into the multiple cosmoses of its past, present and future lives, found itself trapped in the thoughts of its own eternal nature.

In a Segais open to the *sídhe*, the pitiful salmon smolt found its expansive, everlasting, potential nature trapped in the confines of a two-dimensional universe in which the only directions seemed to be 'up' or 'down'.

Once the *cnó* of no return had been cracked open and consumed, the salmon in its *sídhe* nature knew that

33

there was only one direction that really mattered — 'OUT'.

To stay in Segais would be to submit to the limitations of a two-dimensional cosmos, and in the uncharted waters of a *cnó*-revelation, a *cnó*-revolution, a two-dimensional universe in which the only directions were up or down would surely crush the creature under the weight of its own limitations.

The river beckoned. All rivers lead to the sea.

Segais, the pool of initiation, the well of introspection, where the neophyte must be challenged to peer deep into their own core nature, becomes a place of limitation once that core nature, *cnó*-like, has been cracked open. And when the call of the river has been heard, it must be heeded. No creature who has had its *cnó* nature uncovered can withstand the limitations of a pool of only two dimensions. The river, running free and wild, leads to the sea. And the sea opens out into an ocean of possibilities.

The *cnó* nature of the Salmon of Knowledge has been revealed to it. In the deep of Segais, doubt has become tinged with possibility. The *cnó* of no return has a stark revelation for the creature of the silvery light.

'Know thyself in the deep oceans, and if you do, you will come to know that you have never known anything of yourself at Segais.'

And thus we come to two explicit revelations about the folklore of Segais. One relates to the number of spots or speckles on the salmon's back. Every *cnó* that he eats gives him a new spot. The Salmon of Knowledge, the speckled salmon with the countless spots, was being suffocated under the weight of its own *cnó*-wisdom. Segais could not contain this suffocating and burgeoning beauty. Segais, with all its power of transformation, had to yield its fruit. The shell of the watery womb must open, and the amniotic fluid must gush forth so that the newborn creature can be delivered to the river on its new journey into self and selflessness.

And here is the second revelation of the sacred lore of Segais — the well of the nine hazel trees, the one where the salmon first swims, erupts and its waters create the beginnings of the Boyne river. When the river calls, it must be heeded.

There is nothing now that can deter or prevent the salmon from beginning its journey to the ocean. The *cnó* has been cracked open. The waters have broken. A birth must occur. The river must be born, and the smolt must swim free.

The ocean calls.

I will wait and watch for you, Bradán Feasa, on your journey to the ocean.

I will watch for you in the streams that flow down from Sídh Nechtain above Carbury.

I shall watch for your coming in the Little Boyne and where the Yellow River meets the Boyne.

I will await your ingestion at Bolg-Bóinne, the Belly of the Boyne, hoping of course that your passage through the belly of the serpentine river will be a transformative one.

I will wade out into the water at Áth Troim, the Ford of the Liver, where the great Brown Bull of Cooley dropped the liver of white Finnbennach into the Boyne. There, I hope, the silver flash of your passing will resuscitate the bulls of old, so that the Finnbennach may stand proudly at Cruachan Aí, and the Donn Cuailnge may once again graze the uplands in the mountains of Cooley above Dundalk Bay.

I will watch for you at the weir at Bective and in the ford at Bellinter.

Eagerly, I will observe your passage northwards from St. Brigid's Well at Ardsallagh.

On the height of Athlumney, in Navan, I will watch for you. There was once a ford there — Áth Luimnigh, the ford of Limnaigh, a bare spot of land. High up on the motte at Athlumney, on that ancient bare spot of land, I will watch a thousand of your passings, or maybe ten thousand, and there I might get a glimpse into an ancient world, a green earth untainted by the concrete intrusions of man. Standing at Navan, one wonders what great geological forces conspired here in far-off times to turn the river Boyne dramatically northeastwards.

From here, the final rush towards the sea begins in earnest.

I will see the silver flash in the water at Swynnerton Lodge, and from the top of the round tower at Donaghmore. From there, your run turns eastwards, and I will stand excitedly on the ruins of Dunmoe Castle, the Fort of the Cow — a very ancient name — to witness your rush towards the homelands of my own soul.

At lofty Ardmulchan, I will watch for you.

At Broadboyne Bridge, I will watch for you.

I will be the angler without a rod, watching for your safe passing at the floodgate in Slane. No otter will confound you there. No memory of your confinement in Segais will hook you at Slane. No, from there you must be free to swim to Linn Féic at Rosnaree.

Bradán Feasa, you must come to Rosnaree, for it is written in the stars. At night, if you follow the stars of the Milky Way, the heavenly river Boyne, the Way of the White Cow, you will come eventually to the white pool beneath the wood of the king. There, in dreams, I have seen your coming. There, in dreams, I have seen my own arrival into a hidden world beneath the water. Down there, in secrecy, beneath the great mounds of Cnogba and Síd in Broga and Cleitech, I have dreamt of otherworlds. There are many worlds hidden in the twilight of Linn Féic at Rosnaree. If the Bradán Feasa should come to me in the starlight at Fiacc's Pool, I should be like the serf at the arrival of the king. When the salmon comes to Rosnaree, the world will fall silent,

and the heavenly bodies will come to a halt. Even the river itself will be still when the salmon comes to Rosnaree.

The water of a million rain showers has washed down here. The rain in Ireland does something to you. It washes the patience out of you until you hate it. And only when you have hated it can you really come to love it. It dampens your spirits until you have become like a bog, drenched in ancient oak. In the bog, the oak recalls its former nature, when it was rooted to the earth yet reaching for the sky. How great a pity it is that the glorious oak tree can be reduced to a putrid and uncouth mass, a grim and slimy gunk in a dank, swampy form.

Thus have we been reduced, from lofty beings whose thoughts and hopes soar into the summer sky towards a willing sun, to shadowy beings who fester in the darkness of our own sludge.

But the misty rain that falls in sheets over the hushed banks of the Boyne at Rosnaree is a rain that washes into our very soul. When we deny our own tree nature, that which roots us to the earth but calls us to reach out towards heaven, we rot in the darkness of the swamp of our own dark nature — that which we deny we can become, even as our stumps are withering and rotting and the vitality of our leaf-bearing nature wanes in the evening of our own self-contempt.

THE POINT OF CNÓ RETURN

There is none who shall look to the bottom of the well of Segais.

Why?

Perhaps it is because down there, in the deepest, blackest darkness beyond sight and thought, in the furthest depths of Segais, we might come to see something of our own bog nature. But our tree nature, that which imagines us feeding ourselves from the soil and yet striving towards a heavenly nature, refuses to see anything in the darkness of the bog with which to identify. That bog nature is completely unknown to us. It is like a stranger — unrecognisable.

Our tree nature worships the sun. We reach out towards it. We adore it. We want to grow towards it. And we behold the rain, and it washes down upon our skin, and we drink it out of the earth. And all is good. But the bog nature is in us all. And even if we deny it to the very last, we will be reduced to bog in the final days of our contradiction.

We cannot deny our bog nature. Ashes to ashes. Dust to dust. Atoms to atoms. Rain to rain. Bog to bog. Even if we spend our whole life denying it, our bog nature will eat us in the end.

Down there, in the murky bottom of bottomless Segais, where none shall peer, doubt meets possibility. We doubt that we have a corrupt nature, but we accept the possibility. When we meet that possibility with open heart and open mind — when we see darkness concealed within our own nature reflected in the sacred pool — we begin a great journey.

There is an eruption; a change in nature. We see in ourselves the things we have only seen in others and a rebirth occurs. Segais erupts, and the river of our greater journey begins to be formed.

When we have seen and recognised our own bog nature in the waters of Segais, and our incredulous selves are washed away by the million rain showers at Brú na Bóinne, the point of *cnó* return is reached. We have eaten of the nine hazels. We have cracked open their shells and peeled back their husk. And in the core is something indescribable — the seed of a new life. It is the nut of a new tree. The source of a new journey. The core of the *cnó* is the bog itself. If we eat the *cnó* and ingest that bog nature into ourselves, we reach the point of magnificent possibility.

Swimming in the pool of our own limiting thoughts and beliefs, we might have come to accept the base falsities about ourselves. We might have believed that we didn't emerge from the soil. Nothing so beautiful could emerge from something so foul. Could it?

Where doubt meets possibility, miracles happen.

Those who have heard Amergin's invocation will be ready to witness the miracle at Segais.

'I invoke the land of Ireland!'

What is that land? The body and skin of Ériu? Does it not also encompass the bogs, and the muck and dirt, and the bare rocks and slimy pools? That land, from which so much beauty is born, is a boggy underworld.

The *cnó* that falls into the well of Segais is eaten by the salmon. The *cnó* that falls into the muck, that sees the sun and feels the rain, knows that it will not be limited. It grows in two directions — up and down. Down grow its roots. Up grow its branches and leaves. The salmon, knowing the limitations of up and down, and having seen its own bog nature, ingested in the nut of the sacred earth, knows that it must now follow a different direction — out!

And that release leads to limitless possibilities. The race to Fiacc's Pool is merely a short sprint. The longer journey will take it to the sea, and eventually the ocean. In the confines of the well, and the darkness of the pool, it has dreamed dreams of the ocean. In the moment of its greatest revelation — a glimpse into its own core being — the creature has caught sight of its own limitless and eternal nature. The journey to Linn Féic has begun. From there, in that pool of the Boyne brimming with possibility, the smolt's vista will be opened to an endless and boundless universe.

The cup-bearers at Segais are those who guard the holy of holies. The inner sanctum. The *cnó* inside its hard shell. Under the nine sacred hazel trees, they are the guardians of the magic. Perhaps they are the only

41

ones who have seen to the bottom of the well. And in doing so, they became married to their sacred task.

But there are deeper things, are there not? How far down should you go, in your journey to self-awareness? The self-aware cup-bearers, the guardians of the well, have seen their own lower depths. And, reaching down towards the darkest parts, they attained heaven, the highest reaches.

One of their foremost duties as well guardians is to prevent the king himself, Nechtain, from peering into the depths of Segais. For none, not even the king, can look to its bottom and ever be the same again. It could be said that a death would occur. But what sort of death should he endure, if he saw the deepest parts of Segais?

His wife, Bóinn, approached the well. Walking around it thrice widdershins, anti-sunwise, she aroused its storm nature. The well became a fountain. No — the well became a geyser!

But the real question here is: what did Bóinn endure in the moments of its eruption? Was she quickly and completely overwhelmed? Was the masculine power drowning the feminine? Was this the concoction of some monk, a medieval scribe writing on the stretched skin of a calf? Was it a monk who made an Eve of Bóinn?

She ate the apple.

She approached the well.

It was the woman's fault.

But there is another possibility here. Perhaps Bóinn wasn't overwhelmed at all. Was she undergoing a baptism? An immersion baptism — a birth into a greater iteration?

Having seen into its bitter depths, Bóinn and the water of Segais were reborn, as the river Boyne. The transformation was profound. In order to take on her new iteration, Bóinn underwent a dramatic rebirth.

She was dismembered.

She lost an eye, becoming like the one-eyed salmon, Fintan, the eternal creature who carries all the mythic wisdom of his ancestors through the various ages of mankind.

She lost an arm and a leg. Like Mata, the great monster of the Boyne, she was being torn limb from limb.

This is, on the face of it, a merciless transformation. The white cow, who sometimes appears in myth as a white mare, is being sacrificed.

White represents innocence, peace and purity.

These things — innocence, peace and purity — are being sacrificed in the shadow of the water. For there, in the shadow, are the opposites of these things — knowledge, contention and contamination. And as the white skin of the cow is ripped open, the blood spills out and the fleshy parts are revealed.

The white cow is dying.

But what is being born?

It is a violent, watery birth. A powerful fountain sprays from the depths, spewing water high into the air. Bóinn is engulfed. Bóinn is transformed. From this moment, mythological history begins. That which has been concealed in the depths is now released into the high air. That which could not be known is now revealed.

The initiate is to become the goddess.

The innocent fish is imbued with perspicaciousness.

A river of knowledge cuts a new path through a barren and nescient landscape.

A new myth cascades down from Sídhe Nechtain and the well of Segais.

A creation myth.

A beginning.

An origin.

A conception.

A moment from which a fabulous concoction of myth and story will emerge.

There is an ejaculation from the earth. It is birthing a river.

The white cow is being sacrificed in the waters of hope and new beginnings.

Creation from destruction.

But who will weep for Bóinn?

Who will grieve for the white cow, cut open by the torrent?

She is being dismembered. She is being dismembered to be remembered. She will give her name to the great river and she will be remembered forever.

How far in your dreams will you go, Bóinn, in order to resuscitate the mythical vision? Will you go all the way to the sea, and then the boundless ocean, so that our dream vision can be released into a limitless and unending sea of possibility?

Mother of the well, with your breaking waters — what is it that is being mythically born?

Without knowing, without dreaming, we are hopelessly adrift. You make us hope-fully adrift, so that we might come to shore in some prosperous land — a land wealthy in myth, a land wealthy in poetry, a land wealthy in music. Such a land would be the wealthiest and most prosperous of all lands.

No, let us not drown in a deluge of our own ignorance, or our own refusal to look to the bottom of the great well. Bring us to the shore of that land that is made of myth, where the sunrises are saturated in story, where there is music in the mists and where the sunset opens to mythic otherworlds. Bring us there and you will have brought us to Magh Mell. Cast us onto that shore and we will honour you forever.

If I float down in that great torrent of water from Segais — that which will always be known as Bóinn or Boyne — perhaps I will drink some. I will imbibe some of that bloodied water. And if I do that, and chew on some of the fleshy parts, will I then become king of my better nature? Will I become the *rí* of my own myth? Will I be fit to rule the untamed waters of my own wild nature?

THE UNBREAKABLE IS BROKEN

If by chance you should cast me up on the shore of the Boyne at Brú na Bóinne, what fortune should this bring to the king of his own wild nature? Should I be a salmon there, ready for the eating? Should I be some morsel, for the birds of the air who congregate on the floodplain of Brú na Bóinne in huge numbers? Or should I be the lost soul, waylaid on his journey from source to sea?

Standing on the shore, looking up towards the rotund mound of Síd in Broga atop the ridge, might I get a glance at my mythical self, in my Samhain dance on the great Brug above Bóinn? Might I see that which I am afraid to contemplate? If my mythical self were to take form at Síd in Broga, what would I be? Would I be the great monster, Mata, being slaughtered upon the stone of Lecc Benn, atop Newgrange? Or would I be Elcmar, in his druidic garb, a mythic and poetic silhouette against the dim and foreboding hues of Samhain?

If the former, what is my crime? What was the crime of Mata for the treacherous punishment of dismemberment at Lecc Benn? He licked up the river Boyne, so that it was a dry river valley. He licked up the wisdom, and the flowing river of myth. He deprived us of the waters of knowledge. Only Bóinn, with her dismemberment, could restore those waters. Two dismemberments. Two creatures sacrificed — the

Mata (Oillphéist) and the White Cow. The river was bloodied. But it would flow with purity again.

We know this in the case of the Mata because, after his killing, the men of Érin threw his dismembered limbs into the Boyne, which presumably was in full flow again following his death. The Mata was brought to his end upon the Lecc Benn, the gravestone on the peak, atop Newgrange.

Síd in Broga is the symbol of all that is eternal in us. It represents that aspect of our nature that is unconquerable. Thus, in essence, the Mata's killing represents the breakable being broken against the unbreakable.

All our fears were brought to nought at Lecc Benn. All our darkest innards were cracked open. Was it that the breaking open of the Mata at Lecc Benn was revealing our own *cnó* nature — the heart of the being, that which is often concealed by the hard shell of our outer nature, but that which survives the smashing of the skin?

Síd in Broga is heart-shaped. If you crack any of us open, you will reveal a heart. We all have one. In the Dindshenchas myth about the Mata, there is no mention of its heart. Just its shinbone and the frame of its chest and its ribcage. In cracking open the *cnó* of Mata at Brú na Bóinne, we revealed that even monsters have a heart.

Síd in Broga was built to last. It could be suggested that it has an eternal, unbreakable nature. The monument endured five thousand years of human history — no mean task. Crucially, and in parallel with that, its myths also lasted through ages of time. Sadly, the Lecc Benn didn't make it. It was removed and possibly broken in the 18th century. But the monument of Newgrange survived almost intact to today. Its form largely undiminished, it speaks to us of ancient mysteries, of soul journeys, and of druidic wisdom.

When Bóinn puts me ashore at Brú na Bóinne, like a fish out of water, I look up at the great *sídhe* on the ridge, the *cnó*-heart of our druid nature, and I catch a glimpse of Elcmar, shrouded in Samhain mist, his cloak wrapped around him, and my heart is greatly gladdened.

He is the living form of the rock that we called Lecc Benn. He is the unbreakable stone of our mythic heritage — that which will not perish at the breaking of the skin and the dismembering of the body. The vision of Elcmar is everlasting. He will not be thrown down, like some broken stone, to be smashed up and used as foundation material for the roads of other journeys.

He was removed from Síd in Broga, so the myths say. Oengus came, on the advice of his father the Dagda, or Manannán mac Lir (depending upon which myth you read) and shamed him out of Síd in Broga. Do we thus admit that Elcmar, the unbreakable stone of our mythic foundation, also foundered?

It is somewhat ironic that in leaving Síd in Broga, Elcmar should retire to the *síd* at Cleitech, across the river. The name Cleitech means a 'stony place'. Elcmar was moved, not broken. Instead of watching the boys at play in the playing fields from Síd in Broga, he watched instead from a more westerly vantage point, at Síd Cleitech.

But I sometimes imagine his shrouded form atop Síd in Broga, eternally watching over Brú na Bóinne, the unquenchable, indefatigable something within us that draws us close to our druid nature.

As a druid atop Síd in Broga, I watched the monster lick up the Boyne until it was a dry river valley.

As a druid atop Síd in Broga, I watched as Mata was broken on my Lecc Benn.

As a druid atop Síd in Broga, I watched with sadness as Bóinn was washed down in the renewing of the waters.

As a druid atop Síd in Broga, I watched my kin go underground at the arrival of the Sons of Míl.

As a druid atop Síd in Broga, I watched as the Bradán Feasa, the Salmon of Knowledge, was brought to shore by Finegas the Wise, only to be eaten by Fionn the innocent, the boy Fionn, Fionn Mac Cumhaill.

Fionn, son of the hazel.

Elcmar left, but in truth Elcmar never really went away.

He is there today, atop the *cnoc* of Síd in Broga, with his fork of white hazel, divining for water, divining for the murky parts that would overwhelm us on our own Lecc Benn.

And here is a question for the wisest of the druids — what lies beneath Newgrange, that can be revealed by the chief druid, forked white hazel in hand?

What, apart from underground streams of water, might he have been divining for?

I once said that I thought Elcmar might be divining souls. Now, finally, I think I know what I meant when I said that.

The hazel stands above the well. The well is the pool of our unconscious. Down there, beneath the *sídhe*, is our deeper knowing; our secrets, yet to be revealed.

No wonder, then, that so many people who come to the chamber of Newgrange in modern times find it such an emotional, life-changing experience.

But what about the breakable that was broken against the unbreakable?

Where is the Mata in us?

Where is the monster, in the morning of our awakening?

Are we born as Mata, or do we become him?

Smashed against Lecc Benn, against the pressings of our fate, our ego lies shattered there, atop Síd in Broga.

There will be no return to the well for us, as Mata.

There will be no return to the well for us, as Bóinn.

Only a return to *Máthair*, Mother. Danu.

Broken as we are, shattered beings of flesh and dust who walk in the hopeless landscape of our own Damoclean morbidity, we shall come to wholeness.

Only that which is broken can be made whole again.

In our remaking on the journey of Bóinn down from Segais to Sea, we will be made whole in a way that only the most perfectly created things are made whole.

Starting out, we thought we were whole.

We thought we were whole until we saw the bottom of the well.

We thought we were whole until we ate the *cnó* of our broken beings.

We thought we were whole until we bore the cups of Nechtain for a thousand nights at Segais.

We thought we were whole until we were brought to Lecc Benn and smashed open.

We thought we were whole until we counted the speckles on the salmon's back.

We thought we were whole until we were torn asunder, our limbs taken away in the great dismembering at the stone on the peak.

We thought we were whole until we stood before Elcmar, and were divined with his rod of magic.

We thought we were whole until we pressed down on the hot blister that rose upon the skin of the Bradán Feasa.

We thought we were whole until we came to the door of Síd in Broga, and were, Dagda-like, refused entry by the new son of god, the one who counted eternity in the passing of nights and days.

The nights come first. It is only in the passing of the longest nights that we can come to the glory of the dawn of our rebirth. And if you enter the House of Elcmar at Samhain, what shall be your weapon — the mirror, the knife or the druid's wand?

Would you offer Elcmar a festive drink — a communal sup — as you imbibe the magic milk from the mether?

Or would you pass him by, the tramp by the road at Cleitech, and think yourself a better man? I thought myself a better man, until I was broken upon the Lecc Benn.

THE FALL OF BABYLON

I was brought to Lecc Benn at 9/11. The planes that struck those towers were the shattered shards of the mirror that my ego could not withstand, piercing my flesh, wounding my sides, like the great towers themselves.

I was about to fall. I suffered my own fall of Babylon.

And the towers came down.

What was left there, except a ruin? A shadow. A corpse. The smoky pit of death. The death of the ego. Those girders. Those huge metal beams, joined in parallel formations, jutting out of the rubble, were like the ribs of the Mata, after his shattering. His 9/11. His 9/11 at Lecc Benn.

The stone axes hewed at his flesh, and hacked at his giant body, like 767s piercing the sides of those towers. The breakable broke against the breakable. There was nothing unbreakable about that day.

Afterwards, the tower of my being collapsed.

Now, years later, the myth of the Mata makes a strange sort of sense to me. The Mata was broken on the Lecc Benn. The Mata became smithereens on the towers of his shattered form. And I fell down, into the burning pit.

And when I think now, about dismemberment, and the limbs of the Mata floating down in the waters of the great river, I think of myself and my own dismemberment.

I can tell you — hand on heart — that for some time after 9/11, I was just about as broken as a human being could be.

I was dismembered.

Every bit of me was shattered.

The disarticulation of my ego might have been the least of my dismemberings.

My shining tower had collapsed into a pit of dust and death and burning, and the ribcage of my shattered being floated away on the waters of apathy. Dismantled, I floated along. I did not know who I was any more. I did not know what had become of me. I daresay several others felt that way too — they did not know what had become of me, after my dismemberment.

My Lecc Benn.

My 9/11.

My Segais eruption.

The salmon was dead. Long live the salmon.

I was engulfed by the dark waters, and they took me down, into the murky depths.

The primordial soup. I read once that that's what we emerged from. In a time before time, long before complex multi-celled, multi-organed biological creatures, there were what one might call singularities. Single-celled organisms. They had no need of dismemberment. They were so infinitesimally small, the earth might not have known they were even there.

Just as we have no way of seeing the individual atoms that make us up, the world had no way of seeing these unicellular creatures.

The unicells could not wield an axe against the earth's forests. They could not take a plough to the rough earth. The could not mine her mountains. They were not capable of being broken down.

They were just there.

They didn't know it, and maybe the earth didn't know it either.

In my dismemberment, my tearing apart, and my journey to the water, I had become a singularity.

Splash, splash, splash, went my bits as they hit the water. But they were not my bits, because I was no more.

As a singularity, you don't hear the splashes of your own awareness hitting the water. Shattered on the Lecc Benn of your own ego's fragility, you fall away, piece by piece, into the primordial soup.

And I imagine now, years later, that if you were to taste that soup, it would be a bitter repast.

That is no soup fit for the Dagda's Cauldron. He might have pissed a less bitter broth.

And so it came to pass that I entered the Boyne. I entered the Boyne as a singularity for my own immersion baptism. But who had prepared a way for me? I made no cry in the wilderness, because as a singularity you have no voice.

In the primordial soup of your first form, voice is a rose in a forest of thorns.

Dismembered, I was washed down in the Boyne.

Dismembered, Mata was washed down in the Boyne.

Dismembered, Bóinn was washed down in the Boyne.

And the soup had a foul and bitter taste.

Bóinn, your eye floated away so that you could not see.

Bóinn, your arm floated away so that you could not grasp.

Bóinn, your leg floated away so that you could not stand.

When you can't see, and you can't grasp, and you can't stand, what's left for you to do except float away in the primordial soup?

As a singularity being borne past Brú na Bóinne in the ever-moving river of your experiences, do you see Finegas casting his net at the weir at Rosnaree?

Do you glimpse Elcmar with his hazel fork atop Síd in Broga?

Do you witness Dagda, entering his new mound on the flood plain of the Boyne?

Or do you pass by, unknowing, into the ocean of your extinguished possibilities?

EVENT HORIZON

Extinguished, I was sucked down into nothingness by a maelstrom at Glenmore, beyond Brú na Bóinne, and the darkness there was like a universe without stars, a universe without light. Einstein might have called it a black hole. Oddly, black holes shrink to a singularity. And beyond that, compressed into nothingness, are vast amounts of material. In the black hole, substantial things vanish into the pit of extinction. Not even light can escape.

One wonders if a thought could find its way out of a black hole. Perhaps it did, when god said 'let there be light'.

Modern astronomers refer to an area in the vicinity of a black hole called an event horizon. It is, in essence, a point of no return. My event horizon was a deadly series of events in a far-off land. The tower of Babylon shook and fell, and a bright day was shrouded with the dust and smoke of catastrophe. That catastrophe was as real for me as it was for some of the people who witnessed it firsthand. A year or two before, I had dreamt about it, in symbolic fashion. I stepped out onto the shore of a beautiful beach, on a day of clear sunshine and blue sky.

I emerged from between leaves of vibrant green, a forest on the shore. Underneath my feet were water-rolled stones of different sizes and colours. The beach was like a Caribbean beach. The sun was high in the sky and it was a beautifully warm day in a tropical-like paradise. The shoreline swept away to the left, arcing to form a small bay. I enjoyed a brief moment of bliss. This was a heavenly scene. I felt like I was in a world before people existed. It was untainted.

But all changed, and changed utterly. In a moment, the sky darkened. The bright sky became a blackened vista, thick with cloud. The heavens opened. It rained heavily. I saw large raindrops hitting the glossy leaves of the tree beside me. As each one pounded a leaf, it was like a great drum skin was being beaten.

The leaves shook off their innocence. The stones at my feet, which had been dry, were now glistening with the wet of a significant drenching. The bright day was gone. A night-like darkness came quickly.

I looked out to sea. It was an angry, brooding sea, heaving with a darkness and a wounded energy. Along the distant horizon, above the line where sea and sky meet, there was a low, flat belly of black and grey cloud. If blue sky was innocence, the black clouds were something indescribable. This was a storm of foreboding — a cloud base of fear, anger and mourning. The gloomy day that had come on suddenly had qualities that were dark and fearsome.

As I looked at the sea, I saw, deep down, two great shadows, two black forms in the depths. What were they, these shadowy forms? I thought, many times in the months that followed 9/11, that those two blackened forms were symbolic of the destroyed twin towers. All that remained after the attacks of that bright, blue-sky September day, were two dark heaps of debris.

Large chunks of the towers jutted out from the great rubble heaps, wounding the sky. Some were parallel formations of great steel beams that had been the tower's ribs, now ruptured and broken; dismembered.

The Mata's ribs pointed skyward.

My own skin was ruptured that day; the skin of my innocence. All my innards spewed out, as the tower of my own illusions shattered and fell. I was, in the days and weeks and months and years that followed, dismembered. I was torn limb from limb and thrown into the water. Piece by piece, the fragments of the tower of my ego fell away. I became rubble. I was in a heap.

The shadows in the water were not just the remnants of two ruined towers. The shadows in the water represented my own coming journey into unknown, gloomy depths. I would have to go down there, into the water, to retrieve something of my broken self, and to piece together the makings of a new world from the remnants of the monster. It was to be a long and lonely journey.

The kings from the lands round about came and placed memorial stones on the mound of the Mata, on his heap of bones.

The Mata was dead.

Long live the Mata.

The Mata would be reborn.

In the ushering in of a new world, an old one would be destroyed. I had to imagine that the sunshine would return to the shoreline of my shattered and ruptured self. It is perhaps fitting in this regard that I should later have an epiphany on a beach in County Louth, a moment during which a tiny sliver of sunlight appeared through the clouds after months of darkness.

Sand. Grains. Tiny rocks and fragments of shell and sea life. A living and shifting thing. There are many more grains of sand on the earth than there have ever been human beings, or are likely to ever be. Walking on sand is like walking on atoms. Every one is part of an overall being.

On that beach, on that day, there came crashing waves of realisation. A tsunami. A tidal wave.

Crash. A thunderous noise.

Crash. An awakening.

Crash. A coming to being.

The wave smashed into me and I shattered into a billion atoms, a billion sand grains, and the beach of my misgivings now stood like a giant cliff face of hardened rock, upon which the great waves of realisation would break, one by one.

If you have heard the noise of the waves, breaking on the starless shore at midnight, alone with your dreams,

61

you will know that feeling that something has crashed into your self-awareness.

At the breaking of the waters, you emerged from darkness to light. The wild, animal nature of the sea had become tamed on the rugged back of your rocky shoreline.

Smash. The noise of plane on tower of concrete and steel.

Crash. The noise of a body of water breaking on the improbabilities of your self-awareness.

Smash. A dismembering.

Crash. A re-membering.

It was all coming to me, suddenly and swiftly, in the night of my remaking.

The monster remade?

No!

Nothing of this monster is a remade misgiving. He saw you, in the pool. In the spawning grounds of your first awakening, you saw the pallid smoke from the towers. You breathed its toxic air. And in the night when the wave smashed against the shore of your misgivings, something gave out. Something of you spewed out, from Segais, a black river; a strange reflection of all that was good in you.

That bright light, towards which you strove, could not unleash a river of darkness. How could something so bleak emerge from something so pure?

THE BLACK POOL

The salmon spawn in the upper pools of the bright Boyne, reflecting only the black of the night sky and not the stars, had given birth not to the Bradán Feasa, but the Mata itself.

In the blackest hour of your longest night, you had seen not Segais, but the Dubh Linn — the black pool of your weakest self, that which dared not strive towards the light but was content, like great tree roots, to plunge deep into the muck and the lower parts of the human experience.

And so the tsunami came. Three great waves hit you. One made you stumble. The second knocked you off your feet. And the third drowned you.

Thrice widdershins you had walked around the sea of your unknowing.

Thrice you had dared to stir the great beast.

Thrice you petitioned Manannán to offer you succour, at your lowest ebb, in the midnight of your black-dark night without stars.

That black-dark, starless night was the inner skin of the crane-bag, the heron's magic offering, cast upon the shore by the tsunami of your listless hopes. You made your way inside that bag, and, finding it empty on the shore of your grief, you were content to let it suffocate you. Standing there, on the shore of your misgivings, all you could see were the storm clouds and the rain and the two shadows in the deep. The towers had fallen and your Segais had become the Dubh Linn. In the Dubh Linn were the ribs of the Mata. Like the lungless Mata, you could not breathe. Breath escaped you and you could not bring it back. The waves only brought water. Water for you to drown in.

O Bóinn, where are the stars tonight?

Where are my bright companions, to carry me through the night?

I looked deep into Segais, hoping to see the starlight, the love-light. If I could see Andromeda in the depths of Segais, I would know that two million years of ancestral evolution had carried me to this time and place. I would see forever. Nothing would dim my hopes. Andromeda, the keeper of soul-light, reflected in the water of Segais, would be a heaven for me. And I could die in a moment, at Segais, staring at the love-light from Andromeda.

Instead, I found myself at the rim of Dubh Linn, with the foul stench of the monster flesh filling my nostrils.

Smash. The first plane had come. A silvery light on a blue-bright day.

Smash. The second plane had come, and a darkness filled the air.

Mata, how were you undone? No great thing falls lightly.

Smash. I hear them crash into you. I hear them hacking at your wounds.

Crash. I hear you rent asunder. I hear you fall. Down there, deep in the stormy sea, I see your dim shadow, that which reflects only the black night that lies between the stars.

MUIRTHEMNE

I missed the constellations.

The stars of my own story, those that sparkled in the eyes of a young boy, and in his own atoms, were like the grains of sand on a beach of lost hope.

But hope returned, like a tsunami, crashing onto the beach of stars undimmed.

The Lecc Benn could claim another victim, but on the day that the great tsunami crashed into the 420-million-year-old rocky shoreline at Clogherhead, something of Andromeda shone in me once more.

I could not forget that, when the tsunami came, the land became known as Muirthemne, the plain covered by the magic sea. So long as I even remembered that name — Muirthemne — whether I recognised the magic inherent in it, I would not founder on the shore of my own grief.

I would not be Atlas at Clogherhead, standing on the shore with the weight of the world on my shoulders. Manannán would bear that burden for me, with the weight of the world on his shoulders and all the great seas beneath his feet.

With so much out of kilter after 9/11, I wondered if the stars themselves were out of kilter. What if all the constellations we knew fell out of place, and were rearranged? What would become constellated in me,

on the shore of Muirthemne? What would become constellated in us, at Inber Colpa, as a people? If not Andromeda, which stars would be reflected in the knowing waters of Segais?

What road would the white cow travel? Who would throw the sun, moon and planets around the sky, if not Orion?

And if the monster's ribs should wash ashore at the Big Strand in Clogherhead, I wonder if they would act as an augmented ford for me, a crossing to another world?

Instead, they found their way to the Liffey, and Dublin — Dubh Linn, the Black Pool. Áth Cliath, the Ford of the Hurdles. And the monster's ribs became a hurdle for me, an obstacle to the otherworld.

So I stayed in this world. And in the shallow pools at Clogherhead, at low tide, I caught my first glimpse of a new constellation, reflected in the waters of my lost hopes. The ribs remained for a long time on the shore. But at night, I would catch a glimpse of that constellation, Constellation Hope, shining like diamonds from the dark obscurity of the empty crane bag.

The rays of a new sun, a new Oengus, found gaps in the clouds and when they made it to earth many things awakened.

Mousikos Hieros Gamos

At Síd in Broga, Lecc Benn was lost. The unbreakable was broken. Its need had come and gone. And a river of gleaming quartz was revealed in its place. On the shore of the Boyne at Inber Colpa, Amergin ('Birth of Song') announced a new song to ancient Ériu.

But what if the new song was really an ancient one, renewed?

What if, when Amergin asked 'who but I knows the place where the sun sets?', I should announce that I had seen the sun rise and set on many a birth of song, but tonight at sunset there would be a new constellation in the western twilight?

What if, when Amergin asked 'who but I knows the ages of the moon?', I should reply that the moon is ageless, and that all he has been counting in his nightly visions are the drooping horns of a cow, mourning the loss of her bull companion?

What if, when Amergin asked 'what land is better than this island of the setting sun?', I should say that there is a better land, beyond the ford of the monster's ribs, but that that land can only be glimpsed among the stars of the new constellation, Constellation Hope?

Would he think me a liar, or would I have to birth my own new song, to equal his?

What would Amergin invoke in me, if not the birth of my own song?

What would Amergin invoke at Inber Colpa? An arrival to new lands?

What would Amergin invoke at Lecc Benn? The passing of the old world?

What would Amergin invoke at Fiacc's Pool? A fertile spawning?

What would Amergin invoke at the Lia Fáil? The inauguration of a new king, a sovereign power over our collective dream?

What would Amergin invoke at Uisneach? A descent into a deeper world.

Would Amergin think it a temeritous act, if I were to invoke the restitution of Ériu and Lugh, at the power points on the Hill of Uisneach?

If I called them back, if we called them back, what would emerge from underneath the sacred stones at ancient Usna?

What would emerge from the navel of my dreams?

What lonely man would walk down the ancient pathways from Uisneach's lofty heights?

Would the Cat Stone roar, if I touched it?

Was it the roaring May fire, burning atop Uisneach for all to see, that brought Amergin to Ireland on Bealtaine Eve?

When he stepped ashore at Inber Colpa, did the ground shudder beneath his feet?

What did Ériu say to him, at that moment of his song-filled arrival? The poet from the south, from a sunny land, whose head was filled with the song of a new birth, and a new arrival, heard a bittersweet song on the shore of Inber Colpa.

The land was invoked.

The sea was invoked.

The stars were invoked.

The creatures of the land were invoked.

The creatures of the sea were invoked.

Vocal chords were invoked.

Invocal chords were invoked.

Amergin sang a new song on the shingle of the Boyne's shore — and as he sang, every grain of sand beneath his feet sang along. Singing that day, that May eve, on the verge of summer, Amergin gave voice to something that had slept since the ice covered the earth.

The voiceless found voice. Even the stones sang.

But what was sweet was also bitter. The Birth of Song had arrived, but the shining ones departed, into their hollow hills.

Was this an end?

Or was it a beginning, in the guise of an end?

'No,' declared Ériu, defiantly.

'It is a renewal.'

And as he walked upon the invoked land of Ériu, Amergin saw the merging of worlds.

That which was above was also below. That which was within was also without. That which had been unspoken was now sung with full lung. No man-poet or bard or musician could hope to fully arrive into Ériu without her fecund blessing.

In invoking Ireland, Amergin was invoking Ériu. In singing his new song, the bard of the Milesians was giving voice to Ériu herself. She was singing through him.

It was not so much a *hieros gamos* as a

Mousikos Hieros Gamos.

And so, *ceol agus craic* was born in Ireland. Music and fun. It was as if they belonged together. *Ceol agus craic* would be wed in a *hieros gamos,* a *banais ríghi.*

When Amergin sang to me, at Clogherhead, and when Ériu sang to me, at Clogherhead, their music was a great awakening for me. I had lost my *craic.* And I had lost my song. I had *craic*ed up.

The question then became 'would there be a return'? Having *craic*ed up, could I make sweet music again? Could such thing even be contemplated? Having left us, would the Tuatha Dé Danann ever return? On my soul journey, which began again in earnest on Clogherhead beach that cold day, it became clear that they had never really gone away.

There would be singing from the *sídhe,* and in the luminous moments of my stupefaction, I would be uplifted. Numb with the sore grief of the killing of the

71

Mata, Lecc Benn would come to me in my dreams as a singing stone.

That which is spoken about is not lost. Myths retold are myths reawakened. And so, myth came to me as sweet sound. There were many occasions when it came to me as a haunting melody, as if a sullen wind were blowing through the Mata's ribs, the harp-strings of the monster.

THE ONE-EYED GOD

Do those who dream of the monster also dream of dismemberment?

Do those who dream of the monster also dream of the horned stone?

Do those who dream of the monster come to place a white stone on the heap of bones of their lost days?

The Mata came and licked up the river Boyne. The Mata came and sucked away all my vitality. The Mata came, and it might have seemed for a time as if the Boyne would never flow again.

But myths retold are myths reawakened.

In our collective dreaming, could we imagine Dagda, with his giant club, smashing the head of the Mata, in the deep? How far down should we go, into the waters of Muirthemne? Should we go where no light can reach? If we should go where no light can reach, how do we prepare a path so that Dagda can shine in the deep? That which is not subject to light can only be subject to imagination.

Down there, in the very murkiest depths of Muirthemne, is a monster of our own making, and no making at all.

Down there, in Muirthemne's secret places, it is quite possible Dagda and the Mata are one and the same thing.

Who can know, who has not brought light to the deepest places?

The journey down is a dour descent. At times, alone in the darkness, you will feel lost. How can there be a way back, out of the depths of Muirthemne?

Myths retold are myths reawakened.

And in my dreams, I saw Dagda, with his great club, diving into the deep waters that covered Muirthemne. What would he recover, of his lost self, by clubbing the Mata in a place where his mind's eye could not see?

Blinded in a lightless place, where no shadows can be seen, how did Dagda find that monster aspect of himself, that monster in the ocean of his own thoughts?

How could he be sure that he wasn't striking at himself?

In the land of the blind, the one-eyed man is king. What about the one-eyed god? What about the no-eyed man? Unless his club had eyes, Dagda was blind in the depths. And yet he found Mata. He found the creature whose form changed constantly, and whose great bulk remained invisible to most.

In the land of the blind, the one with the club of his own courage is king.

For a day at Muirthemne, Dagda was king. (He had long been the king of Linn Féic).

How, I wondered, did Dagda find his own crown in the place where light cannot shine. And then I remembered. I remembered that square hole cut into the rock of the seabed, that mystery portal from which the lava-light flowed. And a great realisation came to me. It is eminently possible, if one is prepared to make the long journey down into the depths of Muirthemne, to catch sight of the lava-light emanating from the seabed of your lost days.

Dagda had gone to the very bottom of Muirthemne, to Síd in Broga itself, and grabbed the light that glimmered from its sacred light box, and made that light shine in the ocean murk so that things that could not be seen were revealed, in all their hideousness and all their pent-up self-denial. Until that moment, Mata was just a shadow, a dream. In that moment, Mata became real. Until that moment, no one knew the purpose of Lecc Benn.

It is likely, I think, that Lecc Benn was made from greywacke, that stone whose widespread use at Síd in Broga means that Newgrange is mostly made of Clogherhead.

Clogherhead, where continents collided.

Clogherhead, where the Iapetus Suture is a sore wound.

Newgrange — 420 million years in the making.

The rock was thrust upwards, out of the earth. And the gods said thanks. The unbreakable was, ironically, made from the breakable. The builders broke chunks of the greywacke off, and sailed the huge slabs down along the coast and up the river, attached to their boats.

75

The builders and their mushrooms. And their greywacke-backey. Something in their visions made them see patterns. They saw chevrons. Zigzags. And, carving their zigzags on the Clogherhead greywacke that became Newgrange, they saw the jagged meanderings of thousands of generations of their ancestors, set in stone.

But nothing about humans is set in stone. We are malleable. Perhaps that is why we ushered in the Bronze Age so enthusiastically. Stone-like, we were stubborn to remaking. But as bronze, we were hammered and formed into something of our own remoulding. In bronze, we could see a future. In stone, we could only see a concretized past.

So the stone builders passed, and the bronze makers came.

Lecc Benn was once in liquid form, a hot substance unbound in the darkness of the earth. Lecc Benn became solid and stood for 420 million years, and more, pointing skyward at Clogherhead.

It probably took just one day to break it off and bring it to Síd in Broga. It probably took just one hour to break the Mata at the Lecc Benn on Síd in Broga. The Lecc Benn was made from ancient rock, thrust up when continents came together, collided. The making of a new world.

Mata was brought to ruin at this stone, but an unmaking was also a remaking. For the chunks of

Mata that floated away did so, like ancient chunks of continent, so as to collide with something else and make a new world.

Did they see this, the druids of Newgrange? When they touched that greywacke at Clogherhead, did it sing to them songs of collision; sounds of collusion? Lecc Benn, the pointed stone, pointing to heaven. All things strive towards the light. Even Lecc Benn could not abide the darkness. So it became the stone that could cast no shadow. Lecc Benn was transparent to its own monster nature. It killed the monster, and it killed the monster in itself.

RETURN TO SEGAIS

The Tuatha Dé Danann brought their four treasures to earth when they came down from the sky. One was Lia Fáil, the Stone of Destiny. But while the legends sing about Lia Fáil, they say little of Lecc Benn. Kings are made at Lia Fáil. Perhaps kings are unmade at Lecc Benn.

Seeing the horned stone at Tara, Queen Tea lay down and made her bed in the soil of the beautiful hill. Seeing the horned stone on the *sídhe* at Brug na Bóinne, the goddess Bóinn foundered.

Segais, my undoing.

Lecc Benn, my undoing.

Rockabill, my undoing.

Bóinn, how do we remake you? When will your continents come together? When will your magma become solid stone?

Mata. *Mo Mhata. Mo Mháthair,* My Mother. Come back to me now, at the place where the tide turns, at Inber Colpa. If you can swim against the current, maybe you'll make it back to the ford of Drogheda. And if you can make it there, Linn Féic is within sight. Gaining Fiacc's Pool, could you dare to contemplate it? Could you dare to dream of a return to Segais?

THE NAVEL OF ÉRIU

Once upon a time, in the west of the world on a misty isle where day is saturated with the energies of yesteryear, a god-like people came down from the heavens and touched the earth at one of its great energy centres. They envisioned Ireland, Ériu, as a mandala, with four great segments each imbued with its own power and its own active nature. The four were held together by an altogether more powerful, more potent, fifth segment — the sacred centre.

This centre is marked by Ail na Mireann, the Stone of Divisions, the Navel of Ireland. The stone is a huge erratic, a block of limestone dropped on the southwestern slope of Uisneach Hill at the end of the last ice age.

Umbilicus Hiberniae. The Navel of Ireland. The Navel of Ériu. Where the sky connects to the earth. Where worlds mingle. Where the Tuatha Dé Danann come alive, in this world or the other.

Ail na Mireann is no Lecc Benn. No monster needs killing on its craggy cap.

Ail na Mireann. My centre. Your centre. Our centre. The *axis mundi,* upon and around which all things revolve. The navel of the great mother, the navel of the earth.

Any being — man, woman, god or goddess — who presupposes to come to Ireland in order to stand at the sacred centre of themselves will never feel the urge to leave it. Arriving in Ireland, from the clouds, in order to come to the sacred centre of themselves, the Tuatha Dé Danann felt no need to ever leave it, so they burned their ships. The Stone of Divisions is inaptly named for those who come to the sacred centre of themselves at Uisneach. It might better be known as the stone of unification.

At Ail na Mireann, the scattered parts of us are brought together. There, perhaps, the goddess shall be remade. Knowing that Lecc Benn is a stone that shattered, and knowing that Ail na Mireann is a stone that unites, which then should we choose when we burn our ships on the shore of *cnó* return?

Most would no doubt choose Ail na Mireann. But what can unite, where there is no division? What can bring together, when there is no separation? The mythic dreamer, in his midnight vision, sees the smoke from the burning ships and wonders why it is that he sees two stones, in opposition to each other, standing defiantly before the gods themselves.

One is transparent to its monster nature.

The other is transparent to its mother nature.

Both are mere shadows in the mist, silhouettes in smoke. But one cannot exist without the other. There is no Lecc Benn without Ail na Mireann. There is no Ail na Mireann without Lecc Benn. In order to stand at the sacred centre of yourself, you must first be dismembered.

The stone of unification is useless to someone who doesn't find themselves divided. And if you cannot see that division, you haven't looked to the bottom of the well. There are none who shall look to its bottom, except of course those who have been disarticulated at Lecc Benn.

When the Dé Dananns burned their ships on the shore, they did so in the full knowledge that they would have to experience Lecc Benn before they could come to Ail na Mireann. Only that divided can be reunified. Or, as C.G. Jung put it, 'only the wounded physician heals'.

Lebor Gabála says the Tuatha Dé Danann landed on a mountain, in Connemara, called Conmaicne Rein. After they landed, there was an eclipse of the sun that lasted for three days. That was the beginning of their shadow-dance, their descent into Segais. They knew there would be no easy pilgrimage to Uisneach, no unsullied way to Ail na Mireann. There were two stones — Lecc Benn and Ail na Mireann — that would mark their journey.

To complicate things, they brought a third of their own — the Lia Fáil. The Stone of Destiny. The Stone of Knowledge. Aligned with the others, Fál formed an Orion's Belt of sorts, the belt of the king.

Only he under whom Fál uttered a cry or a scream could dream of coming to his sacred centre.

Only he under whom Fál shrieked could prophesize the journey to the sacred centre.

Only the listener to the cry of Fál could know that there were three stones, and three sacred centres.

Lecc Benn for dismemberment, a coming apart, a falling away, a death.

Ail na Mireann for re-memberment, for a coming together, a rising to the surface, a resurrection.

What then for Fál, except knowledge — knowledge that the true sacred centre is not a geographical location, a point on a map, but rather that something within you that calls you to your salmon nature, urging you to return to the spawning pools of your imaginations.

Fál is the screech that beckons you to consider your eternal nature, that north star within you around which the universe of your own existence revolves. Fál is the heart of your eternal self, that which cannot be stranded on Conmaicne Rein, that which cannot be burned on the strand of your abandonment, that which cannot bind you to a physical place.

In my dreams, Fál screams in a manner that leaves me unflinched. Fál screams and kings are made.

It puzzles me why, but Lecc Benn comes with gentle song. It makes no raucous din, but rather sings a soothing melody. Such a sweet sound, for a stone that sunders sinew and flesh. The harsh monster is undone by a siren stone.

And in my dreams, Ail na Mireann makes no sound. Silence. Mystery. Mother.

The scream, the song and the silence — this is how Fál, Lecc Benn and Ail na Mireann approach me in the night of my Danann wanderings.

After Lecc Benn, I needed to go to Ail na Mireann. Uisneach would reunify those things that were torn apart when the wind rushed through the ribs of the Mata and the sound of my death drifted on the air.

Ail na Mireann, do not divide.

Ail na Mireann, do not divine.

Ail na Mireann, mother stone, remake me.

There was something indisputable, in the pressing nature of their task here, having landed on Conmaicne Rein and burned their ships in the west, for the Tuatha Dé Danann.

'We must come to the sacred centre.'

'We must come to Uisneach.'

'We must come to Ail na Mireann.'

And every challenge that they met, whether at Maige Tuired or Finntraigh, would be met spiritually at Uisneach, would be met psychologically at Uisneach, would be met psychedelically at Uisneach. Uisneach would be their Ail na Mireann on the Isle of Destiny. The heartland of the heart isle. The centre of all things.

The Tuatha Dé Danann burned their ships at Connemara because they knew — and they had seen it in their dreams — that Uisneach would abide even if the world should end, and the sky should fall. Ail na Mireann wasn't just unbreakable — it was eternal to them.

The Navel of Ireland. The Navel of Ériu. That indescribable something that connects us to all eternity. No wonder then that the goddesses implored Amergin, Birth of Song, to allow the land of Ireland to be named after them, at Uisneach.

THE OMPHALOS SINGS

The lost pilgrim, coming to Uisneach and connecting with its power points, sees the omphalos and knows that there are worlds and universes within him that have not yet been explored. When Saint Patrick arrived at Uisneach, it is said that he saw a hag there — a *cailleach* — and she was practicing black magic. He took a hold of her, and with mighty power he threw her so that she landed in Lough Derravaragh, miles away. What Patrick did not realise is that this hag represented a world within him that he had not explored. Refusing to explore it, he threw it away. But something of his own hag nature would never go away.

We may fail to recognise that hag world within us. We may refuse to acknowledge its existence. But it is there all the same.

The hag never left Uisneach. The hag never left Patrick. She just called him down, to some place that he refused to travel. Knowing that Patrick had circumvented his own hag nature, she lived in him all the same. She lived in him to await the day when he would finally see her. She lived in him to await the day when he would finally acknowledge his own hag nature.

She would be a *bean sídhe* to him, or a virgin by the shore. Either way, he would not be able to throw her off. With siren song or startling screech, she would come to him as his own dream image. He would see a man,

85

but that man would speak only as a woman. She would comb out her hair at the river's edge. Naked, her paps glistening with the water droplets of a Derravaragh untainted, she would call him to his own hag nature. Refusing to see it, shielding his eyes from the siren, he would behold a despicable change.

Her cheeks would sag, her hair would turn white, her skin would dry up and wrinkle and her teeth would become yellow and jagged. She would offer him a drink, from the well by Derravaragh's shore, and he would refuse.

Patrick would utter a curse upon the woman, so that she would be banished from Uisneach and banished from his dream visions. But cursing the hag is like throwing a handful of sand at a charging boar. She is impervious to cursing. She is transparent to banishment. You cannot banish something of your own core nature. You cannot banish something of your own hag nature. The *cailleach* endures all storms, come saint or sinner. And the omphalos sang to Patrick.

Making his bed at Uisneach, Patrick was a stranger to its rocks and trees. He slept on the peak, away from its power points. Sleeping alone on the top of Uisneach, Patrick dreamed of his own pagan nature, that which he banished in others but could not drive out of himself. The cadaverous hag would come to him, and offer a drink, but he would flee in terror. He only had the tortured man for company. Seeing the omphalos at

Uisneach, I trembled with excitement and trepidation at the multiple worlds within me that were yet to be explored.

Ériu, bring me home.

One question pressing upon the neophyte at Uisneach could not be easily answered. As a goddess, could Ériu be quartered at the navel? As a hag, could Ériu be quartered at the navel? As a maiden, glistening with the untainted waters of Darravaragh, could Ériu be quartered at the navel?

Touching her own navel, could Ériu feel the centre of herself, that which was at one with the heart-centre of the cosmos? If so, the gods would surely abide forever. If not, they would surely pass in a day.

The quartered goddess can only be unified in five fifths. There is no other way. Patrick's way was a tripartite way. There was no room for a fourth or a fifth, and no room for a hag. Three-fifths does not make a whole. The whole can only be found in the belly of the woman.

Patrick should have hastened to Derravaragh, to the swan lake of his dreams, to petition the maiden at midnight. Instead, he slept on bare Uisneach, in the wind, with only the tortured man for company.

Twisting and turning in a restless and fitful sleep, Patrick beheld a vision of the Cailleach in a dream that was worse for him than anything he had seen previously. The hag offered him her breast.

'Suckle me and you will be nourished,' she said.

'Suckle me and you can re-enter the womb through my belly-button.'

He refused, of course, but was forever after filled with a morbid curiosity that he could never confess to another. He wondered what might have happened, if he had suckled the hag.

Spurned at Uisneach, cast away from Uisneach, she would never appear to him under the daylight sun again. She became a lady by the wayside for him, a moving statue in the thickets of his dreams. Sometimes he would see that statue, right before him, her legs splayed and her vulva wide open, and he would jump up breathless and sweating in the night air at Uisneach.

As Sheela, the hag was cast in stone in her most potent pose — an image that, once seen, is seared into the mind. Refusing to kiss her, and refusing to suckle her, he would be offered only full-on fornication. Mouth, paps, omphalos, vulva: she offered each of them, so that you could be made whole at Uisneach. The five-fifths. Refusing each, your tripartite ways would be a cross to bear on this earth.

No one could now come to the navel of Ériu who had not been broken by the phallus of Lecc Benn. Lecc Benn, the stone that sat for centuries above the cruciform chamber of Síd in Broga, would be your cross to bear. You would have to be crucified first, on Lecc Benn of the cross, before your journey to Ail na Mireann could begin. Dismembered at Lecc Benn, my

five-fifths found their way to the Stone of Divisions, that which magnificently unifies.

Ériu, bring me home.

THE ETERNAL MAN

On the green slopes of Uisneach, there was a man, a pale pilgrim who had made several circuits of Ireland and who looked as if he had been knocked apart and pulled together several times. I watched as he passed St. Patrick's Bed on the peak, and walked down the slope of the hill in a southwesterly direction. Shortly, he came to Ail na Mireann. There, at its side, was a guardian. A woman, of course. This was no Nechtain's Well.

She bade him welcome and asked him why he had come. Lifting his hat from his head, as if in respect, and bowing slightly, as if in obeisance, he said that he had come to Uisneach because he had seen every other part of Ireland and, beautiful though the whole land was, he could never find his own centre.

One night, in a dream, he said he had encountered an old woman who asked him for a kiss. He obliged willingly, and after their lips parted, she pointed to her belly. 'Find the navel,' she said. 'Find the navel, and you will find the centre. That which has been divided will be unified.'

He said he did not know what she meant, but months later he heard two men at the side of the road talking about the 'Navel of Ireland'.

'What is that, and where can I find it?' he asked them.

'That is Uisneach,' one of the men replied, 'where Ériu lives.'

And so, the pale pilgrim related, he knew that he had to come to Uisneach. Passing St. Patrick's Bed, he knew, as one who had been broken, that the place of his remaking lay not on the summit, but in a nook on the slopes.

'Can I go in?' he asked the guardian.

'Go in where?' she replied.

'Can I go in through the navel of Ireland?'

The woman smiled. Passing by her, he stooped down, as if looking into the great stone. It was three times his height. After a few seconds of furtive searching, he was soon flat on his belly. The tall man had become prostrate, like a crawling creature of the earth. Perhaps this was the proper way to approach the great goddess. Within moments, as the guardian watched, he found an opening under the great stone and crawled in.

Lying on the flat of his back, on the sacred earth beneath Ail na Mireann, the pale pilgrim found that the confined space of the fissure in the rock was just about big enough to allow him to lie there, and to converse with the stone.

The stone had no voice, but those seeking their centre find that it has a way of talking.

Underneath the great Navel Stone, the pilgrim had a vision of himself in an altogether different form. He saw himself as an eternal man, one who does not perish, and one who cannot be undone by dismemberment. He saw his very atoms fuse with the earth. And after they

had fused, they were released again, and he took a new form. The one who had been undone at Lecc Benn, several times over, was being remade at Ail na Mireann, the navel of the goddess, the navel of Ireland.

Mother, how do we remake you?

Bóinn, how do we remake you?

Ériu, how do we remake you?

First, you must remake yourself. In the dark crawl space under Ail na Mireann, the pilgrim reached his hands upwards, to touch the great stone's underbelly. Doing so, he expected to feel the weight of the earth pressing down upon him. Instead, the stone felt light. It felt like he could push it away with his hands. Under Ail na Mireann, the pilgrim became Fionn mac Cumhaill, able to cast stones around the landscape of his mind with ease. As he lifted the stone, it seemed to him as it all the burdens he had carried on his many circuits of Ireland were now as light as this great rock.

He was pushing at his own contradictions.

He was pushing at his own retributions.

He was pushing at his own inflictions.

Refusing to push back, they were instead losing their gravity, so that they became light, so that they could be easily pushed away.

Under the navel stone, universes were joining and separating. Worlds were merging. Resting on the belly of the mother, he wondered if, in coming to her centre, in coming to his centre, in coming to the centre of

Ireland itself, he would enter into her womb, in order for a rebirth to take place.

In the darkness behind his closed eyelids, he found that his eyes were very much open, and suddenly all the things he had seen in his expeditions seemed like such trifling and inconsequential occurrences. At what point, he felt he was being asked, had he said or done something that had merged the worlds? Merging the worlds, he had thrown the boulders of his guilt away. He tossed the boulders of his transgressions. Fionn-like, he had removed his burdens to the far shores of Ireland.

He threw his boulder burdens east, and south, and west, and north, far from Uisneach, and far from Tara, and far from Gullion. Cúchulainn-like, he grabbed the great Tathlum and threw it around the sky. The many places of its landing would mark the graves of his regrets. Dying there, under the setting moon in the soil of Ireland, his regrets would pass into another world, a world beyond judgement.

Free from the Tathlum of his regrets, he could balance the giant Navel Stone on the tip of his little finger, if he so wished. On the earth, merged with the sacred soil of Uisneach, he laughed as the weight of Ail na Mireann diminished to that of a grain of sand.

Behind the closed eyelids of his very open eyes, he beheld a great navel. There was an opening, like a portal of spirit and light, circular but narrow. As it dilated, there emerged a giant stone globe. Rings of light flashed and pulsated, emanating from the navel. A new world was being born. A new world, in which the dim light of Andromeda reached to the bottom of Segais, was coming into being. A new world was being born in which the old mythic giants were the night beauties of someone's love dream.

Fionn walked there, in the light of the world being born.

Amergin walked there, in the light of the world being born.

Áine walked there. Brigid walked there. Ogma walked there. And Nechtain walked there.

In the night dream at Omphalos, the Tuatha Dé Danann rejoiced in their decision to burn their ships at Conmaicne Rein. There would be no need for ships, no need for escape, no need for retribution, no need for absolution.

Ériu had called them back, to the heart of themselves. Like a bird in a tree she watched them, and her morning song was a sweet calling, a lulling to a deeper place.

Under Ail na Mireann, the pilgrim shook. There was a great vibration, as if the earth quivered at the burning of the ships. The pilgrim lost his grey and dusky pallor and instead he became like an amber sun, shining a bright dawn into the long night of his many journeys.

Ériu heaved and breathed beneath him. And they smiled. Conmaicne Rein became a mountain of declaration, of determination. Burning their ships at Connemara, the Tuatha Dé Danann knew they only needed to come to Uisneach to find their centre. Coming to their centre at Uisneach, they would never leave Ireland. Ail na Mireann is where their sky nature merged with their earth nature. The fusing of their natures at the Navel of Ériu was a calling, a calling to the world.

LUGH'S BED

Lying in his bed at Uisneach, I wonder how Lugh is connected to the earth. Had he fallen down, into the pit, at the coming of the Milesians? Had he lost his many-gifted nature? Could his long arm reach into the unfathomable depths of his own fallibility and there bewilder the Milesian ships with a storm of his own crafting?

Lugh, son of Eithne.

Lugh, son of the earth, son of the mother, son of the *máthair*, did you carry your burdens into the earth at Uisneach? Or, elevated to super-god, did you have to carry all our burdens as the Dé Dananns went down into the *sídhe*?

At Uisneach, Lugh Samildánach became Lugh Chromain, Little Stooping Lugh. The Samildánach had become Atlas, with the world on his shoulders. They descended into Ireland from the sky, but now the Tuatha Dé Danann went into the earth. Aerial beings cannot be contained in caves hewn out of rock. Unburdening themselves of their surface duties, the Dé Dananns went underground. There, under the hill of Uisneach, Lugh found that the beauties of that surface would come to him in dreams. He dreamt of pathways cut through bare rock, pathways to otherworlds, pathways to the surface world. And it haunted him.

In his dreams, he would see sun and trees, birds and clouds. But in his waking hours, the weight of Uisneach, and thus the weight of the living, breathing world would press down on him. Lugh the many-gifted had become Lugh of the burden, with the world bearing down upon him.

Diminished, he became hidden from us.

Diminished, even his name became obscure.

Diminished by the ever-increasing burden of a Milesian world, Lugh became something else. He became Lugh Chromain. The Leprechaun.

In my dreams, lying on Lugh's bed on lofty Uisneach, I have seen down into a deep and narrow tunnel hewn through the rock. Leading down, and down, and down, it takes me to places I haven't been, to places I don't want to see. On the flat of my back, on the stone heap at Uisneach called Lugh's Bed, I have seen that narrow shaft, that dark duct through the rock, the one that leads to Lugh's burden.

Strange the tale, but it seemed to me that only someone who had looked into the dark tunnels of their own nature could lead their burdens into the cracks and crevices there found and hope that the sun would shine on them. Seeing that narrow tunnel, leading downwards into a darkness that faded to the deepest black, beyond where light could shine, I felt fear, but I also felt curiosity. Could I go there, even if the sun can't go there? What fell shapes might greet me, in the deepest crevices of the rock under Uisneach? If I shouted down into the narrow tunnel, would Lugh hear me? What would I say to him? What, from my own burdened life, could I say to Lugh to restore his Samildánach nature?

And then, as I lay on my back on Lugh's bed, a remarkable thing happened. Trance-like, I entered the most relaxed state of mind and body that I have ever experienced. I might have been under hypnosis for all I knew, but every limb, every muscle, every cell in my body became relaxed. It was an idyllic state. I could feel my pulse slowing. My breathing was effortless.

I felt as if all of the anxious moments of my life raced away from me and I had become blissful such that I was no longer having the experiences of a mortal human being. In the twilight, stretched out upon the grass-covered rocks, I looked off into the clouds of the sky and felt that I might be looking at a different universe, a different creation, millions of light years away. There was another me, in a far-off cosmos, and I connected with him. For a few moments in the twilight at Uisneach, I was on an Uisneach that was beyond the reach of human dreams and mortal thoughts. No one in their right mind could ever believe that an ancient pile of stones could make a comfortable bed, and yet there I was, the son of Eithne, lying on the bed of Lugh, son of Eithne, at Uisneach of the stars.

A special blanket was wrapped around me, a blanket of immortality. For in those moments, I was cocooned from my mortal life, and a covering enfolded me — a veil that imbued bliss. It wasn't that fear or anxiety or envy had been removed. It was more a case of those emotions never having existed in the first place. And I said, there and then, that if I was to die at that moment, on that spot, that it would be the most perfect death anyone could wish for.

For the first and only time in my mortal existence, I was prepared to die. Realising that great understanding, many things suddenly became clear.

The beds of Irish archaeology (there are lots of monuments called beds, from the Irish *leaba*) are not mere tombs and burial places. They are the places where the gods went down to rest. And in going down to rest, they ventured off to other worlds, far-off realms, distant cosmoses and unknown universes. And all the time, they had the ability to come right back into this world, if they chose, without a moment's delay.

This is an essential facet of the *sídhe*, that magical Irish word that describes (or attempts to describe) such ineffable places. These are places that are beyond the reach of ordinary human experience. No wonder, then, that the scholars of archaeology refer to them as tombs. They are dead things. They have no vitality. Humans were put in them, after death, to rest eternally. And there are no gods.

But the archaeologist of the soul, having sunk a trench and dug deeply into his or her own core spirit, sees that the human existence is but a phantom, and that the real and undeniably vital animated being is the one who exists in several universes at once.

The cocoon, the shroud that enfolded me at Lugh's bed, was in fact the Féth Fiada, placed carefully and tenderly about me by Manannán. Not so that I would be concealed or kept apart from the world of my conscious existence, but rather because this moment of great realisation was personal to me at that time, and so the great energy of it had to be contained, lest a great and brilliant light should emanate from Uisneach and be seen by mortal eyes at many miles distant. Their time, hopefully, will come too.

It is very bold of me to say this, and I beseech the compassion and patience of the Tuatha Dé Danann if I utter a falsity, but for the first time I think I understood why they seemed willing to relinquish Éire, their Ireland, to the Milesians. They had encountered themselves in other worlds, other universes. They saw themselves reflected in the stars and constellations of a far-off cosmos and from that point onwards, *sídhe* became a word that no language could rightly or accurately describe.

Had Lugh not seen that? Surely one of the great Tuatha Dé Danann luminaries couldn't have been denied that glimpse into Tír na mBeo, the Land of the Ever-Living Ones. This was another of the things that became clear to me. Lugh Chromain was just one aspect of a Lugh who was very much alive in multidimensional otherworlds. He could shoulder the burdens of carrying the earth beneath Uisneach because this aspect of himself — the burden-carrier — was only one of many. Lugh mac Ethnenn and Lugh Lámfada and Lugh Samildánach are all very much alive and brimming with vitality.

Despite his burdens, Lugh Chromain was willing to assume another great load. At Uisneach, Little Stooping Lugh, encumbered by the weight of his burdens in the deep earth, adopted my burdens as his own. He took them and heaved them up onto his shoulders. He took my fear, and he took my anxiety, and he took my guilt, and my anger, and my self-loathing and my jealousy, and even for a moment my fear of dying.

I lay still on a bed of rocks at Uisneach and experienced a nirvana such that I never could contemplate in my entire waking existence. Lugh Chromain, Lugh of the Burden, took my burden at Uisneach as his own, and carried it into the earth. How am I to thank you? How am I to thank you, except by remembering you?

Myths retold are myths reawakened.

Lugh is the one, I read once, who will lead the charge when the Tuatha Dé Danann come thronging from the *sídhe* to save us in the last great battle — the Third Battle of Moytura?

And so we come to another of the great realisations that stemmed from that state of bliss on the rocks of Lugh's bed — the immortality of the Tuatha Dé Danann is our immortality. They are undying because we are undying. The *sídhe* are not places of death. They are access points to worlds that are brimming with vibrant life and vivid possibility.

I lay down to rest on Lugh's bed so that I could see Lugh in his every form. And Lugh Chromain, the little Leprechaun, winked at me from the slender tunnels cut into the rock beneath Uisneach — shafts and crevices and channels where I believed I could never fit, but which I now realise can be travelled in forms that are not known to us in our waking hours.

FLOURISHING SPRING

Travelling down through that narrow borehole into sacred Uisneach, we encounter something else too.

Water.

At Tobernaslath, the spring of Usnagh, also known as Finnflescach, 'the Bright and Flourishing Spring', something of the eternal nature of the Tuatha Dé Danann gushes forth from deep in the earth. In the lowest and darkest crevices of mighty Uisneach, Lugh and Ériu meet in secret and plot their elopement at the coming fall of man. For man must first fall, before the gods can rise.

In the pure water of Tobernaslath, they bathe in the jealous moonlight, and during such displays of courtship, Lugh banishes his Chromain nature, banishes his burden, and accepts Ériu's offer of a kiss at the well.

Transformed from old, weathered hag grown weary with the years of waiting, she becomes a voluptuous young woman and the two, naked, entwine. There follows a heaving and full-blooded copulation, a merging of their forms. Nothing in their nature is so muddied that it cannot be resolved in the pure flowing water of Uisneach.

The spring water emerges from the depths into the cool air of night under the trees at Tobernaslath, and with it emanates something of the indefatigable presence of the Tuatha Dé Danann, that which cannot be put down or diminished by the refractory insistence of Milesian overlords.

Shedding his burden at Tobernaslath, Lugh emerges as the rejuvenated anchorite, one who refuses the apparent permanence of the ascetic life. Casting off her Cailleach nature at Tobernaslath, Ériu reveals herself to the moon and the stars, and the bare roots of the surrounding trees see her transformed into a young woman who knows every road and byway that will bring her to her hag state.

Ériu is a woman who has come to terms with her every condition — innocent child, potent maiden, she-warrior, starlit siren, incurable nymphomaniac, tender mother, minacious crone. She is no silent partner in a marriage of convenience. Ériu and Lugh are two halves of the same thing — the relentless life force that urges us to strive towards our better nature. Relieved of his burden at Tobernaslath, Lugh regains his Samildánach nature and becomes the one who is lacking no gifts or abilities.

Finding her navel at Tobernaslath, Ériu is centred. Her sky nature and her earth nature and her heart nature become one. She is remade.

Ériu, the mother of all our dreams that strive towards perfection, is remade at Uisneach.

This is how the Tuatha Dé Danann come to the surface for us.

Far beneath Ail na Mireann, and far beneath Lugh's bed, and far beneath Tobernaslath, the water travelled in darkness for aeons. Unaware of its origin or its destiny, the water found its way through rock that was billions of years in the making.

A seed planted in the dark soil will strive towards the light.

The salmon, in a black-dark river, will urge itself onwards, over all the weirs of its diminished nature, and will strive for greatness in the spawning pools in the upper reaches of the river. What had Lugh seen in the black depths of Uisneach except a flickering light, a silver flash, and the first seed of a thought that he would chase relentlessly to the surface? The Tuatha Dé Danann want to return to the surface. There, Segais will overflow.

There is no surface world that can be attained through thought alone. To come to the surface of this world in full congruity with it, and with yourself, requires the acquisition of some knowledge of your own subterranean world — those places where you thought, perhaps, the light could not reach.

Down there, millions of years in the making, is your potential to become a superb surface world human being, the sort that in the past has inspired great and wonderful stories about heroes and warriors and gods, and their fantastic exploits.

105

The Tuatha Dé Danann, upon their return, will be the exemplars of all this, and more. We cannot forget that first they came from the sky. Then they inhabited the surface world. And then they went underground. They are the gods of three cosmoses. Their bravest act of all was to go underground. It was a hero's journey for them, one with a bitter but rich harvest.

GOLGOTHA

Lugh mac Ethnenn became Lugh Samildánach, the master of all knowledge. He had attained the highest realms, had he not, in the king's chair at the great banquet of Tara? What need did he have to venture into subterranean realms? Why did he — Christ-like — take on all our burdens? He endured his own Gethsemane, his own Golgotha, at Uisneach.

Lying down in his bed, his wounded soul went to sleep for us and he descended into the darkness beneath Uisneach. He became Lugh Chromain, the little stooped Lugh who carried all our burdens. He became Lugh Chorpain, the body of Lugh, the little body of Lugh. Spent and apparently useless, he descended into the black pit of our ignorance in a pathetic effort to shine light where light cannot be seen or have any effect.

The god of light would meet his own doom in the tight spaces beneath fair Uisneach. Christ, you died, Christ, you rose again. Lugh, spare us your death in the depths. Do you have to die, in order to rise again? I saw Lugh, Little Stooped Lugh, in a tight spot at the bottom of a dark and narrow shaft. There, he called on me. He called on me to come down to him, and to bring my burdens. He said he would take them from me. I did not wish to compound his suffering. I did not want to administer another lash at the whipping pillar. I did not wish to drive another nail into his bloodied hands.

I did not want to pluck a wreath of blackthorn for his crimson crown.

All I wanted to do was reach down to him and grab his hand and pluck him out of that tight space. But me and my burdens would not fit down that hole. I thought I might be the one to bring Lugh to the surface, but he laughed when I said it. He told me to put my ego away. And so I fell. I stumbled in the way. The towers fell, and they fell on me. The glass and concrete and steel came down on me, and I stooped and stumbled. And I went to sleep in the bed of my undoing, because I could not bear the burdens of the surface world. So I went down into the winding tunnel beneath my waking hours, and as I descended I did so as a man alone, one convinced that he would never find his way back to that surface world. And in a way I was right. I would never return to that surface world. It would change because I would change. So I stooped and stumbled in the dark.

In the going down, into the soil, into the rich greyness of a part of me that was far beyond the sight of daylight, I may not have known it then, but I was bringing a seed. I carried a *cnó*, a blood-red *cnó*, rich with the possibilities of a life renewed, down into the darkness of the grey earth of Brú na Bóinne. I may not have consciously carried it, but it came with me nonetheless.

I thought, at the time of my going down, that there would be no more growth, only decay. A pall of smoke

and dust covered my sun so that it shone no more. Darkness came then, and I was lost.

But there's something about shadow, and the nature of shadow, that cannot be lost on a human being who endures nights and days in the weary world. Shadow cannot exist without light. There is only shadow if there is light, and something to obstruct that light.

The *cnó* taught me a lesson.

Lost to the world, or so I thought, I entered the barren soil of my loneliness, just as one might do at death, in order that one's body be returned to the earth. I was Lugh Chorpain, the little body of Lugh, laid down into the soil of my own corruption at Brú na Bóinne, where I would surely die. But there, in the bare and dusky soil, I saw the *cnó* cracked open, its hard shell parting under the strain of a million years of knowing. The heart-seed was there, in all its reluctant potentiality, the sweet core nature of something that appeared as a dry and desolate, hopeless thing.

From the cracked-open husk, a bright green root emerged. It was first rooting itself, before its miraculous journey to the light. The *cnó* would show me the way back to the surface world.

Stoop not, Lugh, in the burrows of your burden-hill. Watch the *cnó*. Watch the *cnó* as it first roots itself to the earth, and then emerges into the surface world. And watch, then, as it boldly reaches for the heavens. There is nothing so bleak about the soil of your sorrows that cannot be breached by the glorious light of day.

The *cnó* reveals its Danann nature. It is a seed of three realms — the underworld, the surface world and the higher realms. Falling from a great height, it enters the earth and roots itself there for a fabulous emergence. Day by day, the roots and shoots of a new life emerge. The cracked-open shell of the *cnó* is its old life, and the old life falls away as the towers reach skyward again. In the shallow soils of Brú na Bóinne, I cracked up once more.

THE SALMON IN THE POOL

How did the *cnó* fall at Uisneach, I wondered. And then I read, in Acallam na Senórach (Colloquy of the Ancients) that the well Finnflescach, also known as Tobernaslath, shared something very important with Segais.

Oisín, wandering in search of the well of Uisneach, came to the edge of sacred Finnflescach. In the well, he saw eight beautiful salmon flourishing in its pure water. The salmon, according to the story, flourished owing to the absolute seclusion of the place. Oisín fished all eight salmon out of the pool using a basin containing eight sprigs of watercress and eight sprigs of brooklime. He presented the eight salmon to the king of Ireland on the hill of Uisneach.

He was bringing wisdom to the table.

The eight salmon perhaps represented the knowledge of the eight segments of the year, and thus there was a salmon for winter solstice, and one for Imbolc, one for spring equinox, one for Bealtaine, and one each for Samhradh, Lughnasa, autumn equinox and Samhain. The fish of the year. Eat them and you shall live forever.

Caílte, we are told, then arrived at Uisneach, having travelled from Brug na Bóinne. He crossed the Boyne, it is related, at the Pool of Fiacc, where the Salmon of Knowledge was caught. Implicit in the

111

bubbling undercurrent of the story is the revelation that Finnflescach and Segais should be seen as counterparts.

Upon his arrival at Uisneach, Caílte greets Oisín, who presents him with some of the watercress and brooklime. Caílte recognises that these are from the 'Bright Flesk' and asks Oisín if he found any fish in the well. Oisín reveals the eight salmon, and says he will share them with Caílte. The latter is pleased, saying that never before had he shared anything more pleasant with man or woman. What a feast, worthy of eternity.

Symbolically, the salmon represent wisdom and knowledge. Physically, they represent sustenance, for the salmon was an important part of the human diet since Mesolithic times. The salmon offers itself up for eating. The recipient of its flesh will receive untold blessings.

In Acallam na Senórach, we come to see Finnflescach not so much a well as a spawning pool. Otherwise, how does a salmon come to live in a well? But there is no story of the sacred well at Uisneach feeding a river. That story is reserved for Segais.

It was Amergin who later said, 'I am a salmon in a pool, I am a lake on a plain'. Amergin knew that nobody could occupy the surface world of Ireland without first having experienced that great journey into the depths, that spiralling journey that led downwards, to the source of all things.

THE DRUID'S DREAMS

I closed my eyes, and the vision of the boy in the tunnel of light returned to me. He turned towards the sword in the stone. Its silver blade was buried fast into one of the great orthostats that constituted the passage. This same orthostat had deep ridges carved into its surface. As I watched the scene, from a height, it seemed that the boy was standing in the light, the golden light that seeped into the darkness like a wayward son finally returning home for the family feast.

My position changed. I was lowered down, beckoned from the heights by some mysterious calling. I descended into the light, but cast no shadow. My feet touched the ground. The orthostats, like giant guardian hands, were aglow in the light of an ancient calling, bringing them to prayer in the hollow worlds beneath the earth. The boy turned towards me and met my gaze. There was something about his eyes that gave me a sense that he was an aged man, a wanderer who had been on many journeys. He looked me in the eyes and as he did so he cracked open my shell and saw straight into my *cnó* nature. A great groundswell of emotion rose up in me then, such that I felt unsteady on my feet. And I remembered that as a *cnó* bursting forth with green shoots of a new experience, I should first root myself in the earth.

So I did. I put down roots, and I felt strong again. He spoke with the voice of someone who had lived a thousand earthly lives.

'This is my Lecc Benn,' he said, as he reached out and grasped the hilt of the sword that was in the stone.

'This is my Lecc Benn, with which I have pierced the monster. I have wounded him between the ribs and he is dead. The monster has fallen. Will you help me cut him to pieces?'

I nodded awkwardly and even furtively.

'We must cut him up now, and throw his marvellous bits into the great river. And when we've done that, we must bury his bones in a cairn of stones. Are you equal to the task?'

I nodded reluctantly again, but something in my rooted nature assured me that I was equal to the gruesome task.

The boy laughed. He took his hand off the sword.

'There will be no need for dismemberment today. You have seen enough breaking apart. Today is a day for remaking.'

As he spoke, he pointed towards one of the great stones beside me, beckoning me to look at it. I peered at the face of the stone, washed in gold at the coming of the dawn. Its surface was smooth.

'No, look lower,' he said. 'Go downwards.'

I stooped into shadow, and hunkering there in the half-light I caught sight of some patterns on the stone.

'See?' he said. 'It is the stone of your remaking.'

I did not know what he meant, but as I hunkered in the cool air with the golden light shimmering above me, I saw spirals and diamonds and zigzags and circles.

'A great artist has been at work,' said the boy. 'A dreamer who has seen stars and suns and worlds beyond ours has carefully inscribed his wonderful vision into the ancient stone.'

I reached out my hand and hesitantly put my fingers into the grooves of one of the spirals.

'This is the vision of the dreamer,' said the boy. 'The dreamer is the one who has seen the spiralling of worlds, one into the other, and the winding journey of life that sometimes swirls down into the depths, and sometimes meanders up towards the heavens. Incised carefully but deeply into its surface, he has brought his dream to life. In this dream, many chequered lights dance on the floor of the earth-womb, and their music swirls and spirals and weaves a sense of festive expectation for the wayward traveller.'

These were profound words for a boy. Here was a youth who stood before me as *ollam* and *fili*, as philosopher and sage. He was no meek neophyte, stumbling in the darkness. I got the sense that he had seen many dawns, and many dismemberments, and much spiralling of words and thoughts into the pathetic void of a great falling. He spoke again, but this time as

if the old gods were speaking through him, in unison, in one great voice.

'Pause a while at Síd in Broga, O weary wanderer of the year. Stoop low towards the druid's dreams, for the things that make you kneel will elevate you beyond measure.'

'Do not go down there for the sake of yourself. Go down there for the sake of the whole world, and all of humanity. Stoop to the shadows. Bathe in the river of black ink. Swim to the greatest depths of Muirthemne and beyond, and the druid dream will come to you.'

'What dream?'

'Have you not seen it, oh wounded man? Have you not seen the flickering silver light in the river of blackness? Have you not been to the lava-light at the bed of the ocean?'

I did not respond.

'Have you not followed the spiral downwards, to wherever it will go, into the void, to pluck there from the Tree of Life the gold and silver apples? Have you not followed the *cnó* that dropped from the tree down to the bottom of the well?'

He turned towards the sword and placed his hand on it again. There was a stirring in the darkness.

'Will you help me pluck the sword from the stone?'

'I am not worthy.'

'None of us is worthy, but which of us is able?'

He put his other hand on the sword hilt and with all the strength that he could gather he gave it a huge pull. It didn't seem to move at all, but there was a great tremor, a deep rumbling.

'Have you seen it?' he said loudly, over the din.

'Have you seen the salmon in the well? Have you seen the salmon in its spawning pool? Have you seen the salmon at the estuary? Have you seen the salmon in the sea? Bring him to Finegas, and to Fionn, and to Oisín, and they will show you how to prepare him for the eating.'

The earth shuddered around my roots.

Often had I stood, over the centuries, on the bridge at the ford, and watched for the flickering flash of silvery light in the evening. Having tasted the *cnó*, the salmon would for ever more feel a great urge, prompting many incredible journeys.

When the tremor died down, something was roused in the dark. There was a sound of groaning and moving. There were creaking noises and something heaved towards the golden light, but I could not see beyond the boy, with his hands on the sword, into the darkness beyond.

'You see,' he said. 'All things strive towards the light. With your roots in the earth, your *cnó* cracked open and your shell dismembered, do you not also bend towards the light?'

I nodded.

117

A Sword in the Stone

'Will you help me? Will you help me to draw the sword from the wall? It is your task. It is my task. It is our task, upon which all the world is waiting.'

I stepped meekly towards the boy. He nodded encouragingly. He put his left arm out, to bring me close. As I reached him, he looked at me and there was a twinkling there, deep in his eyes, the spark of something ancient. Many suns and many moons were there, and a million stars. Those eyes had seen lifetimes come and go, and lives born and spent, and marvellous acts and grievous deeds.

'Who are you?' I asked.

But even as I asked, I knew that no name, no word or human utterance could hope to vocalise or enunciate this being's gaping depth. I sensed, even before asking, that this was no normal boy, no everyday youth.

'Would it matter,' he said suddenly, 'if I said I was the boy Sétanta, or Diarmuid, or Cormac mac Airt, or even the great Dagda himself, standing in the palace of Elcmar?'

'You are all of these, and more,' I replied, although I did not know why I said it.

He smiled.

'I could be your Birth of Song, your Amergin,' he said, 'in order to name the nameless things, and to give voice to those things that cannot speak, and to bring back something from the glorious past, to allow it re-emerge from the shadows into the brilliant light of day.'

An army stirred in the darkness.

A battalion of shadows disturbed the still and cold air.

There was an agitation. A stimulation. An incitement. A calling. An arousal.

The boy leaned towards me. He looked up at me, wide-eyed.

'Are you ready?' he whispered.

'Are you ready for the rebirth, the reawakening, the resurrection, the renewal, the rejuvenation, the restoration, the resuscitation, the renaissance, the revival? Are you ready for the return?'

With each word, his voice grew stronger until he seemed to be shouting.

I nodded in agreement, but this was an involuntary act.

'Pull the sword from the stone,' he shouted, and again there was a great trembling and shuddering, and in the darkness there was a heaving, and the sound of unsheathing swords and the clanging of shields.

I put my hands around his, on the hilt of the sword, and together we strained to pull it out. After a mighty yank, it budged a bit, but even as it did so the golden light grew to a brilliant glow so that we could barely see. The sword gave another budge and there was a great flash, a blinding light and an enormous rumbling, as if all the creatures of the deep were in stampede, freed at last from some long captivity.

Blinded by the light and deafened by the sound, I fell backwards. I fell to the ground so that I was flat on my back. I felt my head hitting the ground but it did not hurt. My eyes were closed.

THE DREAMER

The earth shuddered and quaked, and there was a colossal din. Behind closed eyes, I sensed that the brilliant light was fading, so I opened them again.

As I did so, the noise began to die down until it rumbled off into the distance. I looked up, expecting to see stones, and the boy, but in their place I saw only the sky. There was a flash to my right, and I turned to look. I could see a huge thunder cloud, emptying its angry rain on the distant hills, and within moments the rumble of thunder reached me, and as it rattled the air around me, I could feel it vibrating in the earth beneath me.

I sat up abruptly. I was outdoors, on a grassy hill, in the evening. The tunnel of stone was nowhere to be seen. The boy was gone. The sword was gone.

In front of me, at a short distance, was a man, sitting on the grass. He had his back to me. He was sitting on the ground, with his legs crossed. I walked towards him, and around him, so that I was standing beside him at a few feet distant.

'Who are you?' I asked.

He turned from his intent ritual and, in a voice that suggested I should know the answer to my question, he said:

'I am the dreamer.'

'The dreamer?'

'Yes, the dreamer.'

'What do you do?' I asked.

'I dream, of course!'

He looked back towards the west, and there in the twilight of day was a new horned moon, framed neatly between the bottom of the storm cloud and the horizon.

'Nothing dies,' he said. 'There is only a return.'

I looked at the slender crescent. It would set soon, before night had fully come.

I turned to the dreamer.

'Sit with me,' he said, gently.

So I sat beside him, facing the moon. He was holding a clay bowl in his hands. When I had crossed my legs, he turned and offered me the bowl.

'What is it?' I asked.

'It is a bull broth.'

I had no idea what that was. I looked into the bowl. It didn't look all that nice.

'It is made from the meat and blood of a bull. Have a sip.'

It looked unpleasant and uncooked. Despite my reservations, I took a sip. It was strangely sweet.

'Many a mighty bull was brought to ground for a sweet feast,' he said.

It went down better than expected.

'Now comes your time to dream,' he said.

'Am I going to sleep?'

'If you wish, but you will find it might not be necessary for dreaming.'

I would have insisted to the old man (who was grey-haired and had weathered features) that sleep was a prerequisite to dreaming, but there was something in his voice and the way he spoke, and even his pose, that reassured me. So I shut my eyes.

There was another rumble of thunder, this one much more subdued and distant than the first, but its sound lingered as it echoed off the hills across the valley. The noise should have unsettled me, but I found to the contrary that it had a calming effect. I had seen no lightning, which was strange even though I had my eyes closed. The thunder gently rolled on for what seemed an age, until I felt the need to open my eyes again.

It seemed brighter. The moon had vanished and the sun was there in its place. I looked over my right shoulder but the storm was gone. I turned around to tell the dreamer, but he was gone too. I took a good look around. The landscape was familiar, but densely wooded. I was sitting on the top of a ridge, in a large clearing around the summit.

To the west, under the sun, there was a larger hill, whose crown was covered with thick forest. I thought I could see the flicker of a flame there, in the trees, and there was a faint smoke rising.

As I squinted to see, I glimpsed, much closer, a woman approaching me. She wore a long white robe, which was hooded, and she had something in her hand. She walked to where I was sitting, stopping a few feet

in front of me so that she blocked the sun. She pulled the hood off her head, revealing a beautiful face and a head of curly blonde hair.

'Are you the dreamer?' I asked her, not knowing why I said it.

'No,' she replied. 'You are the dreamer. I am the messenger.'

From beneath her cloak, she held out an object.

'Here you go. You will need this.'

She presented me with a branch, or rather a twig — a forked twig. I took it in my hand and looked closely at it. I examined it, turning it in my hands.

'What do I need this for?' I asked, looking up, but she was gone.

The fork of white hazel was my fork in the road.

A time of decision.

A place of decision.

Halt a while, grey traveller of the dusk. Pause a moment, on the ridge of the mist-entwined twilight. Those who have passed here before have something to say. They have a lot to say. They travelled far to arrive at the bridge of day, the ford of the night, the causeway that brings day and dark together for the coming of the soul. When everything fades to darkness, and the stars are not to be seen, music and memory are your friends in the night.

THE GREAT RIVER

The best of your memories — those golden moments of your life — are there, like a tune that you once sang or a tale that you once told, ready for the retelling.

Seared into your memory, the mind sings at their recollection.

When the grey dusk comes, and the evening falls early on the ridge, the fork of white hazel calls you to go to the water. You must venture down to the shore of the great river, and plunge your magic stick into the water. It calls you to go there. It demands of you an honest errand. Plunge the white stick into the waters of Bóinn and she will speak to you of all the things she has seen and heard, all the obscure images of your dreams.

My journey from the ridge down to the shore is a sacred one. I should go barefoot, so that I can touch the earth, so that there is no barrier between it and me. In that way, the earth will speak to me. The soil and the stones and the sticks and the grass and the leaves will speak to me. They will speak to me in tongues unknown and their strange speech will greet me as a foreigner in the night.

But on the ridge, prostrate in the moonlight, a vision of their meaning will drown my dreams so that they will be saturated with knowing. The stones will boil with meaning, and in the coming of the new moon I will cook the fish in the *fulacht fiadh*. No man will come to the *fulacht fiadh* who has not heard the stones speak to him, at night, in his dreams.

Alone in the dark, I must make my way from the ridge down to the river, on a starless night, by paths unknown. There is no predefined pathway. No winding trail. The white hazel tells me I must do as it does, and fork at the points of decision, the points of indecision. At each stone, and bough, and bush, I will listen to the earth through the ears of my feet, and fasten my decisions to the sails of the boat of my intuition.

The river forks beneath the great ridge, dividing its flow around the islands in the stream. What makes one drop go right, the other left? In all its travelling, from rain cloud to limestone cave, from mystery well to swelling sea, when did the water droplet know it would go left or go right at the fork in the river?

Thus, like the raindrop, I must go from ridge to river in the blindness of the night. Tonight, on my journey to the river, I will be guided by a different sight.

The stick man dances on the earth.

Left, right, straight ahead.

Left again.

Light-footed, he prances on the bare earth and the ground meets each step with a rapturous welcome.

Step on, step down, walk on, walk over, with a skip and a hop your heart shall ready itself for the adventure.

'Come down off that lofty height,' the river says.

'Come down here and bathe in me so that we shall know each other's dreams.'

In the dead of night, one man walks the earth in darkness while all the others sleep.

Exhilarated, I skip on through the darkness. Never did I think that walking alone in a starless midnight could bring ecstasy. But after many lives walking alone in the dark, the soul yearns for its friendship.

Truth be told, there is something so honest, so truthful, about the dark and if you can walk there, you can surely live forever. Because there is no light there, there is no reflection either.

The white hazel does not reveal its bright nature without sun or moon or star or flame, but something of that bright nature reveals itself despite the darkness. Only he who is afraid of the dark seeks to bring light there. Only those with ceaseless questions spoil the dark with a light of their own making.

And so the careless wanderer asks why, and where, and what, and who, and when, and how.

But what is the last question?

What is the only question you should bring to the darkness, when you've extinguished your candle and put away your torch?

What does the night traveller need to know of the darkness? It is this:

when did you and I become one?

In becoming one, we have no need of torchlight. With only obscurity and the ears of our feet to guide us, we listen. We listen for that sound that is the most precious of sounds for the human journey on the earth.

We listen for running water.

Descending from the ridge, we shall find our way to the ford by the precious voice of the river. And as we get closer, even the stick will speak.

The hazel divines water. It will lead the way. Quivering and jolting in my hand, the fork of white hazel will lead us to the great queen of the waters. From ridge to river, we will arrive as kings remade.

No descent was ever so glorious!

I would stoop low towards the druid's dreams, so that a great elevation could take place.

'Stoop low,' says a voice, and I imagine that the hazel wand is talking to me.

'Stoop low, but towards your own dreams. Be the druid. Be the dreamer.'

A stick snaps beneath my feet, and its cracking comes as a great noise, breaking my stride.

I pause for a moment.

I take a deep breath.

We are close.

Walking forward now tentatively, I find there are bushes and undergrowth around me. I put out my arms to brush away the foliage.

The water is loud. I am almost at the shore.

The river runs fast and my feet will take me there with the acquiescence of the earth itself. No darkness, no obscurity, can shroud the sound of the great flowing river.

I take one more step forward, and the bush gently touches my hands and legs, and as I pass through I am there.

I can feel its potent sogginess in the soft clay beneath my feet.

I have come to the river, and the river has come to me.

This moment has been tens of thousands of years in the making.

Stepping forward slowly and gently, I allow the trickle of the water to delicately caress my toes. I look down, not expecting to see anything in the darkness, but suddenly there is light because the water sparkles as it passes over my toes. I look out across the great river and it offers a magnificent reflection.

I see, down there, the skies of another world.

There is a myriad stars, glinting and glimmering, and it seems to me as though the river has great depth, a deepness beyond the measure of the mind. Looking up, I can see no stars. The clouds still obscure the night. But in the water, in the depths, I see familiar constellations.

I see Cygnus.

And I see Cassiopeia.

And I see Orion.

They move, like a host of moving things, in the depths.

There is a magnificent world, down there, if only you would explore it.

The stones of the river bed, polished and smoothed by ten thousand years of watery action, and more, have seen it. They have come to know themselves as the stones of another world, another creation altogether. In our world, they see only the reflected possibilities of that reality. And in their world, they have come to know the river intimately.

They wash in her, every day.

They drink in her, every day.

They drown in her, every day.

And with the coming of each new morning a distant sun dawns on the nascent dreams of the fathomless oceans of the world.

As I stand at the river's edge, in the dark of night, watching the skies of a distant world beneath, I feel the smooth stones under the heels of my feet and I feel as if I should tell them that I know them.

'Hello, old stone,' I might say.

'Hello, ancient traveller of the many-earthed world,' it might say in reply.

If I pick it up, it is likely that I will recognise it. There is something about us — me and that water-rolled stone — that, being both composed of the stuff of the earth, we are one and the same. We are bonded in a sort of ancient material familiarity.

A stone is only inanimate in your world if you dream it so. But in its own world, it is imbued with limitless possibility. In its own world, perhaps it is a living and breathing thing.

THERE IS ONLY A RETURN

What becomes of us when we die? The physical parts of which we are made do not vanish. They live forever. As atoms. Who wants to live forever? Our atoms, those tiny things that we cannot see in ourselves, survive all corruptions. Something of us lives on. Something material. Something animate.

We are only dead when those last bits of us are brought to nothing, smashed and destroyed. And even then, there is the soul.

It may be that, at the moment of our physical, corporeal death, something of us is released to share an ecstasy in many other worlds and realms and deep and high places. When my physical form breaks down, and I am no longer animate in this world, and my pen is at rest and I cannot stand at the shore of the Boyne to greet the dawn, what will become of me? What hope should I have, that I am only animate when all my constituent parts animate me together?

Heraclitus said that when a man returns to the river of his younger days, no matter how familiar it seems, it is utterly changed. For he is not the same man, and it is not the same river.

And so, gazing down into the glittering swirls of water beneath my feet, I see reflected in the stars and constellations of that other world a real hope that, post-death, I will become manifest in many different realities.

The pen might not move in this world, but the words will flow in many others.

Maybe, like a tidal river, those words and thoughts will flow backwards and forwards, upstream and downstream, so that my song and my story will reach the ears of far-distant ancestors of the past, and far-distant progeny of the future.

In that way, their *amher-ghin*, their birth of song, might be mine too. We will share our birth of song across many generations. Each new generation that comes along might, I hope, come to the river's edge and pick up the smooth stone and tell it 'I know you'.

In this way, none of us will ever have to die. And so the words of the dreamer come to my ears like a soft melody, carried down from distant hills by the great river, one that says: 'Nothing dies. There is only a return'.

And who should know this better, except the great river herself, whose water droplets have travelled to the top of the highest clouds, and down into the deepest caves and crevices of the earth, only to be born again in the dawning of a new life at the well, the holy pool?

There, at Segais, the watery wanderer issues forth from the darkest night into the most glorious day, and the cycle begins all over again. Animate in another reality, the smoothened stone of the river shore tells me that all is well with the ancestors. They too paused in the way to say hello. They too had their Amergin, their birth of song, and found coming alive that which previously they had no words to articulate or sounds to sing.

Tonight, in the waters of the great river beneath the cloud-obscured ridge, there would be a great symphony. All the stones would sing.

I should bring these stones, these precious smoothened rocks, up to the ridge, and pile them up in a great cairn, an inanimate heap of stones that will sing for the ancestors. They will sing of the otherworlds they have seen, reflected in the waters of the great mother river.

That is the dream.

I stand there, feet in the water, with my fork of white hazel in my hand, the other hand keeping my cloak about me, and I turn my gaze from the deep worlds of the pool to the world above my head. At that moment, there is a parting of the clouds and a bright beam of pale white light shines down.

A waning crescent moon appears through a gap in the clouds. Beside it, close by, is the bright Morning Star. The cow and the calf shine together, in the river of the sky. The Way of the White Cow. And the way shall be known to the dreamer who comes to the river by paths unknown.

I hold out my precious fork of white hazel, reaching towards the sky until the moon sits atop one prong and the Morning Star sits on the other. At that moment, I am Fionn mac Cumhaill, the Starry Son of the Hazel, and it becomes apparent to me that although I am a child of the earth, born to walk on its ever-changing surface, my gaze is fixed on the stars, and my dreams take me upwards, towards the heavens.

Amergin is there.
Lugh is there.
Danu is there.
Fionn is there.
Bóinn is there.
Oengus is there.
Elcmar is there.

By the power of my hazel wand, I will fling the moon along its path through the stars, like a stone from a slingshot. With the holy hazel, we will reckon days and months and years. But we will do much more. We will divine water. And we will divine souls. The many universes will be revealed to us, the diviners on the ridge above the great river. The ancestors and the progeny will meet us there, at the opening of a great doorway into the many-hewn realms of possibility — the doorway of the dreamer, he who casts many chequered lights into the pathways of possibility.

Cupping my hand, I stoop down, hunkering towards the river. I place my hand into the moonlit water, to catch the droplets of moonlight and the river that is

135

born in every moment. I bring my hand to my mouth and, standing again, I take a sip.

'The wounded man has come to the shore,' says the voice.

'The dreamer has come down from the ridge. The diviner has found his way to the river by dark paths. The pale pilgrim has come to be revealed in the moonlight. A great birth of song is happening. Nothing will ever be the same again. In the night of your druid dreaming, the goddess has been awakened.'

I had a compulsion to bathe naked in the water. So I did. I stripped off my clothes and, carrying only my fork of white hazel, walked into the river. In my naked honesty, I would bear all to the river. There is no lying to the river. The river sees all. The cold water reached up to my chest as I waded out into the deepest part. I was not afraid. I held my arms out. The hazel stick was in my left hand and I held it up over my head. The mud of the river bed squelched beneath my feet. When I had reached the deepest water, I stopped.

The river glistened in the moonlight and it struck me that dawn would not be far off. If there was to be an invocation and a rebirth, it would be an honest and modest moment.

THE WHITE-CLAD LADY

I spoke to the river.

'With your leg, I shall stand. With your hand, I shall write. And with your eye, I shall see. Mother river, you who have been to distant shores and lofty sky-tops, wash me here now in the stream.'

And thus it was that I, naked as the day I was born, was baptised to a new life, the life of the dreamer.

I plunged the white hazel into the water, or maybe it forced itself there, and for a moment it was as if a great current was running from the water into this holy implement and from there into my veins.

I closed my eyes but even as I did I felt a great trembling through my body and visions flashed and pulsated behind my closed eyelids. In my quaking visions, I saw flashes. There was a lady, clad in white, illuminated briefly by the lightning. She was holding a small dog. Without speaking, she told me that she had come down from the well for me, and for all others who would honestly and earnestly follow their dreams. In my nakedness, I was not ashamed.

'I have come down from the well,' she said, 'where you were not afraid to look. Only those who have looked to the bottom of Segais, or those who swam to the bottom of Muirthemne, can know of what I speak. You went down there, to the darkest depths, following

137

the *cnó* after it dropped from the living hazel wand, and long after you lost sight of it in the darkness, you kept going down. Many others would have given up, but you were relentless. Even your doubt died there in darkness. But before all hope was allowed to fade, you saw it. You saw it down there at the bottom of all darkness.'

'The lava-light!' I shouted, with much excitement. And even as I said it, I was under the water, and I could see the lava-light, and so I swam down to it, to catch it with the hazel fork. I plunged the twig down into the water until I caught the lava-light on it. Drawing it upwards, I found that it illuminated the river for me. It was like a great torchlight in the waters. I thought about coming to the surface, but something kept me down there. Just before I ran out of breath, I saw it. I saw the flickering silvery light of something that flashed past me, through the water.

I surfaced with great commotion. It was as if all my surfacings had come at one moment, following a thousand submergences into the deep.

'The salmon!' I said, gasping with exhilaration. And as I looked down into the water, I saw another silvery flash, and another. They were swimming upstream, against the current. They were, I imagined, returning to the spawning pools, and a feeling of elation welled up inside me such that I felt my heart would burst. My *cnó* nature was wanting its own revelation, here in the river

of my remaking. Another silvery flash passed through the water. And another, Soon, they were relentless.

'Rise, O gentle son of the morning, with your wounds healed and your spirit renewed.'

Even as she said it I knew the woman with the dog was likewise rising, with healed wounds and a body recomposed.

Mata.
Mo Mháthair.
My water.
My mother.
Bóinn, are you remade?

Have you come back for us now, at the place where the tide turns?

I received no audible answer, and I could not see her, but something in the water that had no voice let me know that this was no Dubh Linn, no dark pool. This was Fiacc's Pool, where dreams are born and myths are made. This was a place for the arrival of the great Amergin, the birth of song.

Bóinn had come down again, from Segais, to be remade.

The salmon were racing upstream, towards the spawning pools of the imagination, and the dreamer who had brought the lava-light out of great darkness was experiencing a dramatic and naked rebirth.

I moved towards the shore. There was a golden glow from the white hazel. The flickering darts of light were shimmering speedily through the water.

I must hasten to the ridge.

Day is coming.

THE FLASH OF SILVER LIGHT

The night of the *amher-ghin* at Fiacc's Pool brought dramatic illumination to the clouded forms of many dreamless nights. On my way back up to the ridge, I thought about all the cloudy days and nights in Ireland, and how often I had pined for sunlight or starlight in the long, drawn-out dreary days of the winter of my barren soul. What would move me from my winter bed of hibernation except that beam of golden winter sun in the hallway, or the hope, when curtains are drawn back and blinds are retracted, of seeing a sky filled with shining stars?

I would revel at the sight of the midwinter light, creeping across the floor, illuminating all the floating dust in the house. There, the detritus of the dead parts of our living bodies would be lit up in splendid joy at the coming of the warm sunbeam. Those bits of us that had been shed, cast off our skin, were now free in the air and ready for the next journey, wherever that might take them. Kneeling in the shade, I would as a child watch those floating specks of me — and others — dancing joyously in the shimmering sunlight.

It is perhaps a miracle of nature that on the shortest days, when the sun is at its lowest, it has the longest reach. For a moment, the cold tomb of the house would dazzle in the golden glow of a reluctant day, and everywhere the dust of our former beings would dance and sing, singing a song of freedom. Those were the forever moments of my young life. Such moments were equal in awe to seeing the Milky Way from the darkness of the countryside, or watching a sunset, or witnessing the arrival of the first swallows in spring.

At other times, the birth of song would come at the close of day, in winter, when the eternally grey sky would, for a short time, become imbued with shades of yellow. And somewhere in the world, you knew someone was watching a rapturous sunset, a sunset so beautiful that it might be the last sunset ever to be seen by human eyes. Under the greyness of a dreary day, you would find your soul alight, as if a warm flame had been set in the hearth of your dusky dreams. And though night would follow, sooner than normal in the quickening shade of a cloud-filled sky, your heart would be aglow in the knowledge that the sun would make a fabulous return.

Standing at the bridge over the ford, I had seen that sun of someone else's world set gloriously upon a life so powerfully charged with optimism, despite my own world being so hopelessly draped with a veil of pallid grey. While darkness was descending for the Tuatha Dé Danann, the bright knee of the warrior bard was seen shining in the ford.

'What land is better,' he would ask, more in declaration than in questioning, 'than this island of the setting sun?'

The one who stands at the ford of night and is witness to the flickering flash of silvery light is the one who knows the glory of the last sunset over the land of men even in a land where such scenes are often obscured in sombre shade.

There is no grey dusk in the heart of the poet. There is no leaden gloaming, no pallid end of day for the one who sings of new beginnings even as the dank grey day sinks to cheerless black.

In the bleak sky of winter's close is the rose-coloured hope of the poet who has fished in seas both barren and abundant. Nothing dies. There is only a return.

Amergin, hook for me a silver fish at Rosnaree.

Amergin, hook for me a birth of song at Fiacc's Pool.

Amergin, hook for me a song of joy at Inber Colpa, so that in the dust of my dreams new hopes will be constellated among the glittering specks of that which I had believed had fallen away.

The poet and the warrior will stand in the ford to greet the day, whatever it should bring. A song must be born at the dawning of the day. It is in such moments that the earth is renewed, and all our darkness is cast off. But while the poet sings a new song, in the ford at daybreak, the warrior must also stand fast, lest the darkness return and plunge the day to gloomy dusk.

The salmon passed here on their way to the ocean.

The salmon passed here on their way to the spawning pools.

Which should we fish for, us anglers of hope and expectation, except that which yearns for a deeper life?

Choose one. Pick a salmon, as he streaks by in the ford under the bridge. Which one would you catch, except the one who has the Milky Way on its back? That is the one whose *cnó* life is older than all of us; one who has seen many sunrises and sunsets at the ford. One who has seen many deaths at the weir. One who has swum in the deepest parts of Segais, and the widest parts of the open sea. One whose flickering light has been reflected in the eyes of many a hungry fisherman. One who has flown through the free air under the watchful eye of the otter or the heron at the floodgate of Slane.

And what then, after the catching, except the cooking and the eating? Be careful not to burn your thumb while cooking the fish. Be careful not to burn your tongue while eating it. In your dreams, the salmon will come and speak to you in the ford beneath the shining bridge.

'What would you do,' he might ask, 'if you should catch instead an arm, a leg and an eye under the bridge in the shallow ford of the poet and the warrior?'

'Would you cook them and eat them too, in the hope of dreaming of a goddess remade?'

Standing in the ford, we might also witness the great chunks of the Mata float by, being borne towards the estuary by the current, like an unfathomable dream that is brought out of the intangible muck of our night visions.

We might see the monster's ribs, or the monster's shin bone. Should we also wish to see the Mata remade?

We worry, do we not, that we don't know which one is which? Is there a difference at all?

Bóinn. My Mother. *Mo Mháthair.* Mata.

Was it Bóinn who was heartlessly smashed on the Lecc Benn? Did we kill that which was feminine in ourselves when we took the Mata to the Lecc Benn for the great dismemberment? Only the men of Erin were involved in that task. The women had no part in it.

And afterwards, when the body parts were being borne downstream by the relentless Boyne, did we not wonder if we had killed the wrong monster?

If the dismembered parts were washed back up again to Brú na Bóinne, what would we wish to see remade there, at the turning of the tide?

QUICKENING STEPS

The journey back to the ridge was perhaps more effortless than I might have expected. Re-clothed and renewed, I was light of foot across the rocks and soil and grass of the incline from river to ridge. Every stone spoke to me, each one in a different language, but every one in words that I completely understood. One said:

The dreams must now be dreamt,
The stones must be turned and returned,
Quickening steps to the hearth,
Where the bones of many will be burned.

The first of the early twilight was making its presence known. I could see the ground beneath me, and the ridge was crowned with a blue-grey hue. I thought of the hazel wand. Yes, I still had it with me. The branch from which the *cnó* had grown before it fell into the water. The white forked branch that gave the salmon its *cnó*. The branch whose light would make many things be seen.

As I hastened from the river, I thought of great circles of stone and wood. A grand scheme. A cosmic vision. All of the land between the ridge and the river was like a great amphitheatre. Someone on the top of the ridge looking down towards the river could witness a great spectacle.

Of all the things wrought by the ancient druids, the circle was the one closest to his own eternal nature. With circles — set in stone and earth and wood — he could carve magnificently the cyclical nature of all life into the surface world, and in doing so he would be hoping that the point at the centre of all things would be the place where this world would open to others.

Every circle has its centre, every hoop its fastening point, every rotund belly its omphalos. The cup and ring would be seen on stone, but it would be set religiously, and with utmost care and devotion, into the earth itself.

I crossed a bare field, barefoot, following the stones of an unknown pathway, like a religious zealot, to something on the ridge which hadn't even entered my conscious thoughts.

Where was I going?

I did not know, except I had a feeling that it might be to the centre of all things; the centre of myself.

Quickening steps to the hearth, where stones would be turned and returned. Circles of stone and wood there would be, to fasten our own eternal nature to the capricious surface world.

The light-keeper had been the light-finder. Somehow, the magician with the magic hazel wand had found a way to do what he had thought impossible. Sinking to the bottom of the ocean, faced with that mysterious square aperture in the bedrock, from which all the light

147

of another world was emanating, he had found a way to submit to the edict:

'You have to go in there'.

And so it was that Lugh, the great and magnificent Samildánach, shed all his magnificence in the pit of his longest night and became the Leprechaun, the smallest of the mythical creatures, so that he could enter that narrow tunnel hewn square into the rock beneath mighty Uisneach. He went down there, to places that he could not see, and he mined jewels for us. He found the diamond in the coal pit. Washing the carbon in the first birthing of Tobernaslath beneath Uisneach, he had found our diamond nature.

Bringing that to the surface for us would be akin to the Tuatha Dé Danann spilling back out into this world.

It would be a quantum moment.

That which is concealed beyond sight will have a glorious revelation.

That would be a fitting day for Bóinn to be remade.

In your worldly wanderings, if you should spot a lonely face, in the starlight, then stop in your tracks and genuflect, and stare a moment in marvel at that wondrous thing that has been diminished and burdened, for you shall not know at what hour or moment that fledgling will become the god or goddess it knows itself to be.

Nothing dies. There is only a return.

OENGUS ÓG

In circles, the one who brandishes the fork of white hazel dances his way back towards the top of the hill, and the salmon run is in full flow beneath the growing dusk of morning.

Somewhere, in another world, there is a great movement. This is a binary system. There can be no breaking through of this world to that one, without an equal and opposite breaking through to this one.

In the growing light, there is a strange ritual. I see dancing and I hear music. Hooded strangers, bedecked in bear furs, dance and swirl with fiery embers. There are characters in their midst who seem uncomfortable there. The hooded ones carry burning branches, swooshing and twirling them to a trance-inducing rhythm. The sparks and embers fly from the ends, creating a fiery show. The shadows moving in the centre of the din are two elders. They are feeling the heat, and must move constantly in order to avoid being burned by the falling embers.

I move closer, enthralled by the curious spectacle. The wooden branches glow red and yellow at the ends. I can feel the warmth, even from a distance. I dare not move any closer, for fear of being burned. The hooded figures are energetic in their movements, which seem to become more frenetic as the tempo of the music increases.

The movement of the elders slows in pace. Soon, they join hands and embrace. Squatting onto the earth, they sit still under a fiery shower. They will surely burn.

But as I watch, they meld into one grey shape and, beneath a torrent of sparks and cinders, they crumple and dwindle into a pile of ash.

The hooded figures stop dancing and the music dies until there is just one sombre drum beat. One hooded stranger stoops to the cinder pile and reaches towards it. He picks something up. He holds it aloft. In the pale twilight of the coming dawn, he reveals it to the others.

It is a bone. An ashen-grey bone. A human bone.

Startled, I slouch down, hoping not to be seen. But it is too late. The hooded figure turns towards me. I cannot see his face, but he paces quickly in my direction. I have nowhere to run. I crouch down in terror.

'Here it is,' he says, loudly. 'Here, take it.'

'I don't want it,' I reply, terrified. I cover my face with my arms. I await the inevitable. Slumped on the ground, cowering beneath his looming form, I imagine at any moment I will be burned alive or meet some other horrible doom.

'Here, take it,' the voice says once more, but I ignore it, hoping that he will leave me alone.

'Why are you afraid?' a young male voice says.

I lower my arms from around my head and open my eyes.

Standing before me is a boy, a slender blond-haired boy with a smile on his face and a warm glow in his eyes. The hooded figures have disappeared; the burning embers are gone. All that remains, other than the boy, is a smoking pile of ashes in a large stone bowl.

The ridge is soon crowned with golden light.

The sun is rising.

'Do you recognise me?' the boy says, staring lovingly into my eyes. He takes my hand and I rise up from the ground onto my feet. I stare at him, and even as I do I know that I recognise him. He speaks again, and as he does so it moves me to tears.

'Pause a while at Síd in Broga, O weary wanderer of the year. Stoop low towards the druid's dreams, for the things that make you kneel will elevate you beyond measure.'

As I hear those words, I weep. It is a weeping of great joy tinged with a sadness — a mourning for lost days and wayward wandering.

'I am Oengus,' he says as he places his arms around me and embraces me.

'I am Oengus Óg, the Young Son, the one who was conceived in the morning and born between that and the sunset of the same day.'

'I know, my son. I know.' And as I hug him, the tears flow like the stream of water that trickles over the rim of Segais, birthing the Boyne.

'Did you pull the sword from the stone?' I ask him.

'As surely as you went to the bottom of Muirthemne and retrieved the lava-light from that mystery portal in the rocks of the seabed. As surely as you followed the *cnó* downwards into the deepest parts of Segais to find the Milky Way on the back of a fish. As surely as you conversed with the lapdog on the shore of Inber Colpa. As surely as you relieved us of all our burdens at Lugh's Bed on Uisneach. As surely as you brought the monster of your own shade to the Lecc Benn to be dismembered. As surely as you have stood on the bridge at the ford, watching for the flickering silvery flash of the first salmon run of the season. As surely as you saw the crane-bag emptied of its delights as the tide retreated at Traig Baile. As surely as you have heard the wind whistle between the ribs of the Mata at the Black Pool. As surely as you have brought the light of the moon and the Morning Star out of Fiacc's Pool with your slender fork of white-bright hazel.'

'Yes, I pulled the sword from the stone, but I had the help of a mighty ally in doing so. In fact, I had the help of many.'

I looked at him through tear-filled eyes. The sun spilled its light across the valley and in a moment many things were revealed.

'I had help, from you,' he said, pointing at me, 'and about a thousand others, people who were willing to go beyond the fright of night and venture into the deepest darkness of themselves. All salmon, rushing upstream to the spawning pools of their first imaginations.'

We were standing in the clearing on the top of the ridge, and the treetops were painted in hues of golden orange and yellow, as if a sudden warmth had come into the world that was never felt before.

It was a crowning moment, when lowly pilgrims of the grey hours were made kings and queens in the high air of a place so sacred that the spiralling worlds would open to each other here in a symphony of jubilation.

'Those who have mined gold and silver, and diamonds, in the deepest places are those who will be crowned here with the jewels of their own self-discovery,' said Oengus, smiling broadly.

'They will be made kings and queens at Síd in Broga.'

'I have no wish to be a king,' I said to him, hesitantly. I did not wish to spoil the air of exultation.

'You shall be the king of your own heart,' he said, placing his hand on my chest, 'and you shall be king of your own mind,' he added, pointing to my head. 'What better kingdom to rule than your own heart and your own mind and your own soul?'

He spoke as one who had fished in many pools of the river of his own soul, one who had been washed out to sea dismembered and come back again, renewed with the incoming tide.

'Oh I have been far beyond that,' he said, and he turned towards the rising sun and his face glowed like someone from the oldest age, as if he was the first human ever to witness the glory of dawn.

I turned with him and faced the sun, and there was a feeling in the pit of my soul that grabbed me then, a feeling that such ecstatic moments were accessible to all human beings, if only they would go earnestly and bravely after that flickering light within the darkness of themselves.

And I wondered if, somewhere in the world, those thousand others were witnessing their own brilliant dawn as the newly crowned monarchs of their own eternal souls.

Would they come here? Would they come to the ridge? Or would they, lost in their own moments, proceed down lonely ways, because one who has been in the shade of themselves does not know how to bring that shade to the surface in others?

After the sunrise, would there come an eclipse?

Doubt is such a human thing, and it comes even in rapture. Should we leave the ridge alone, so that it would not become crowned with a thing of our own making, a vestibule to some other way?

Leave the earth as it is. And leave us as we are. The earth will be better for it, and we will be better for it. Give to the earth what is earth's and give to man what is man's.

Let us go back to the forests and the streams and the shaded uplands.

Mata, we tore you apart at Lecc Benn. We tore you apart so that a new world could be made. But it is a folly, because man did not make the world, and man did not make himself. Man cannot unmake the world without unmaking himself.

What have we done, except broken the monster only to remake another? We have heaped stone on stone, and bone on bone. Should we dare to call this a triumph?

'You do what you do,' says the boy, saturated with the colours of dawn, 'because remaking the monster is the only thing you know how to do.'

'But why. Why do we remake it?'

'Because that is the gold that you mine, the diamond from your deepest shafts and crevices — the will to make something better with your own monster nature. Nothing is so dark that a light cannot be made to shine on it.'

I thought about my own jewel, my own precious thing. It was no nugget of gold or shining diamond. It was a slender, Y-shaped twig, a piece of white hazel that had once been part of a tree growing over the sacred pool at Rosnaree, the hazel that had grown from a blood-red *cnó*, dropped at the pool's edge by some sage of the ancient world.

In the first dawn of its breaking, it sundered wonderfully, rooting itself in the deepest world of itself while its soul sung to the stars.

As I grasped it, in the flourishing dawn on the golden-green ridge, I knew it to be more precious than any coloured stone retrieved from the bosom of the earth. It was, to my mind, a living, breathing thing. An animate object, capable of communicating things which had never been uttered using spoken languages, or written in words.

The starry son of the hazel was both warrior and bard — the one who stood waist-high in the water of Linn Fiacc, waiting for either battle or poetry. He was equally ready for either, but in any event he was to find that the hazel branch was a more powerful weapon than any sword, in the right hands.

HIGH SHIP ÉRIU

Amergin, were you born to the song of a warrior?
Amergin, were you born to the song of a poet?

In the glittering pool of your first iterations, did you speak as a poet-warrior or a warrior-poet?

Were you undecided between sword and words?

Or were you, Spanish interlocutor, stuck between worlds, between the world of the warrior and the world of the poet, like a fish out of water at Inber Colpa?

Landing there, on the shore where the Boyne meets the sea, was there something of your own forked nature that revealed itself as you first put your foot into the river's precious waters? It is said that ancient poets were often imbued with inspiration on the verge of water, especially that of a sacred spring or river. What elevated you there, at Inber Colpa?

When you stepped into the Boyne for the first time, what was it in the water that had cascaded down from Segais that spoke to your poet nature, and what spoke to your warrior nature?

You were the one to whom had been communicated the secrets of the quelling of Dé Danann ire, the one who had been given the keys of the surface world of an undying Ériu-land.

After the dusk of that first day of your arrival to the Island of the Setting Sun, what stars shone for you in the pools of the great river, the Way of the White Cow?

You were my Fionn, in the waters of Inber Colpa.
You were my Elcmar, in the river where it meets the sea.
You were my Fintan, shining in the way.

It was a brilliant thing that you did, coming around Ireland to land at Inber Colpa. You were seeking the ways of the goddesses. Your brother, Erimón, harried Ériu. Your brother, Eber, sought for her. But you, Amergin Bright-Knee, the one who brought the birth of song, spoke to Ériu as the poet at Uisneach, seeking not this, and not that, but listening to the wishes of the goddess.

If only you would allow that name, Éire-land, to become its name forever, you would be granted access, through poetry and song, to the heart of the goddess at the navel of Ireland.

Then came the judgement, at Royal Tara, another place where a goddess rests. At the beautiful ridge of Tea, you said you would leave, over a distance of nine waves, and you were true to your word.

And even when the storm came, at sea, you cursed not the goddess, but chose again to seek to return

poetically, in your boat that was named the 'High Ship Ériu'.

Invoking Ireland, beseeching Ériu, petitioning the goddess, you calmed the storm, when the others only wanted war. You put the warrior away, and arrived as the poet.

But your best was yet to come.

Sailing around Ireland left-hand-wise, widdershins, in the same way that Bóinn brought the Boyne into being at Segais, you came to her very own waters, at Inber Colpa. In that way, you came to meet her on her own terms.

The place named from the leg of the Mata, the shinbone of the great monster that was undone on the Lecc Benn on the ridge above the sacred pool, was the place where you would plant your leg on your second arrival into Ireland. Planting your leg poetically at Inber Colpa, you would become the tree that would bear fruit forever on this enchanted island.

Perhaps the leg of Bóinn would be there also, at Inber Colpa, so that your disembarking would be a homecoming and not a wily incursion.

Placing your foot on the shore of the Boyne at Inber Colpa, you could stand in the absolute truth of your being — that which declared itself to be harmonised with the creatures and plants of the wild world, notably the bull, the vulture, the fair flower, the boar, and, most significantly, the salmon.

You declared yourself to be the salmon in the pool at the estuary of the leg of the beast; the leg of the goddess.

But even this was not your finest moment, which was still to come.

Lebor Gabála says that you arrived into Inber Colpa on the seventeenth day of the moon, at Bealtaine. There must have been something extraordinary written in the stars that day, on the day that you melted the hearts of the goddesses and brought the birth of a beautiful song to the shore of Ériu.

Who but you knows the place where the sun sets?

Who but you knows the ages of the moon?

Who calls the cattle from the House of Tethra, and upon whom do the stars of Tethra smile?

As the stars rose out of the sea on that brilliant day, there was another constellation of shining things in the waters of Bóinn, a myriad flashing lights that signalled your elevation from poet-warrior to druid deity.

I would have gone there myself, and placed the shining fork of white hazel into your hand as a token, and an emblem, and a key — the key to the secrets of all arcane knowledge, and the key to the songs of the heart, and the tunes of the soul that would be sung on the hilltops and at the lake-sides and in all the high and low places of Ireland for ever more.

I would not have been worthy of laying it at your feet, but it would have been my great honour.

BIRTH OF SONG

I had been searching. It was a noble but seemingly fruitless quest. For years, I had laboured towards some glint of knowledge, something to indicate why you seemed to have such a welcome place in my soul. For two long decades I searched. I sought that knowledge in the books and ancient stories of Éire.

What was it about this bright-kneed Spanish bard that kept the candles of my own poetry lit, and that brought me to soul-singing in the damp and dingy hours of the winters of my fruitless labours?

When I was a child, growing up, I remember that I could look out obliquely through an upstairs window of the house I grew up in and I could see the old cemetery of Mornington village. I was fascinated by this. I would take my small telescope and shove it through the narrow opening in the window, just to watch the traffic passing on the road beneath that graveyard.

That telescope was an instrument of the dreamer and the poet as much as it was the apparatus of a scientist. There were many stars to be seen through that little telescope, and it must have been the case that I looked beyond the twinkling points of light, into the darker areas in between, to see what lay there in the interminable spaces that separated us from our shining hours.

I might have seen Amergin landing there on the shore of the Boyne at the little village of morning, and if I had done I doubtless would have seen the cattle of Tethra called forth to dance in the heavens above his holy head.

Only years later did I learn about this very auspicious landing, this disembarking that came at a moment of great change not just in the Boyne Valley, but in all of Ireland.

The gods gave way to the mortals, but Amergin was no ordinary mortal. Like Fintan, he was ever-living. He ascended to the status of a god. Much like Oengus, and Dagda, and Bóinn, his name would be remembered as long as there were humans living within reach of the Boyne.

Amergin is ever-living because his song lives on in us, those who feel a calling to the Boyne, a calling to sing at its merry shore the ancient songs of a world never forgotten.

I have a *grá* for the Dananns. I am tantalized and mesmerized by their shining nature. Being creatures of the sky, and the deep earth, and the surface world, they would appear to be the fullest expression of the complete human — one who is willing to re-enter the cave because it holds no fear for them.

But all the time while I walked in the blue air by the Boyne, and even the red and ruddy hours, and in the darkness, this figure known as Amergin Glúngeal was by my side.

Twenty years it has taken me — more than a Metonic Cycle of the Moon — to come to a great realisation.

Amergin was the astronomer and the poet, the scientist and the wordsmith. He could count the ages of the moon, but more importantly he could commune with the goddesses, who saw no threat in him, despite their own looming descent into the *sídhe*-world.

In the waters of the Boyne, at Inber Colpa, perhaps he had seen his anima personified as Bóinn remade. Any mortal man who can commune with the goddesses is made immortal.

Now, in the 21st century, I remember the Milesian poet of Bronze Age mythology as a dear and ever-present friend. And I wonder, if I returned to that old house of my youth, overlooking the Boyne, and looked out through that window with my telescope, if I wouldn't receive a great affirmation — a vision of the past, standing in the water, making his vivid and beguiling incantation.

Would he stand there, on his bright-kneed leg, as the poet of the new dawn? Would he stand there, on Bóinn's leg, as the druid who had retrieved the golden light of his own feminine nature from the deep seas of his masculinity? Or would he stand there, on the leg of the Mata, as the one who had retrieved his own monster nature from the darkest recesses of his human soulscape and, bringing it to the surface, had embraced it as a long-lost friend?

Twenty years I have been searching — not a month less — for that birth of song. And now I find that it has burst forth in me, like a fountain. That's over seven thousand sunrises and sunsets. But who's counting, except Amergin and I?

Amergin, birth of song.

Bóinn, birth of river.

Long was thy coming foretold. The soothsayers had seen it. Ériu had seen it. And she told Amergin, 'yours shall be this island for ever'.

Singing your song, in the water at the harbour of the Boyne, something came to you, like a flash, like a bolt from the blue. This was your greatest moment. Declaring yourself to be the salmon in the pool, you invited something — something that could aptly be described as a great ejaculation. As a poet, you had reached a moment of poignant and stunning climax, and all of nature was with you. There, in the birth canal of the Boyne, where the tricklings of Segais become the vast open sea, there was, in your own words, a

Cassar find.

A white hail. A bright lightning-flash. Your flash of inspiration.

It wasn't enough that you arrived as a wind on the sea, an ocean wave, a powerful bull, a hawk on a cliff, a dewdrop in the sunlight, a fair flower, a brave boar, a

salmon in a pool or a lake on a plain. That might have been enough for another poet, but the birth of song in you pushed you further; pushed you to say:

Íascach muir!	A fishful sea!
Mothach tír!	A fertile land!
Tomaidm n-éisc!	An eruption of fish!
Íasc fo tuind	Fish under wave
I rethaib én!	Streams of birds!
Fairrge cruaid!	A rough sea!
Cassar find	A white flash
Cétaib iach	Hundreds of salmon
Lethan Míl!	A broad whale!
Portach laid—	A harbour-song—
'Tomaidm n-éisc,	'An eruption of fish,
Íascach muir!'	A fishful sea!'

The fishful sea delivered its fruits into the river mouth in a tremendous torrent — an eruption, a bursting forth, a white hail, a bright flash.

And now, a great homecoming is occurring. The salmon who left the Boyne as smolts are returning to the spawning pools. The druid-poet has called on them with his harbour song and they are ready now to go back to start the next cycle. There is a substantial influx. Amergin is imploring a deluge.

THE CORMORANT

We don't understand why salmon know how to return to their natal rivers and pools. We just know that they do it. Perhaps it is a salmon's intuition that brings it back to the place where it was born — something that draws it to return to its own beginnings. I have no doubt that these magical fish are also following sun, moon and stars on their journeys.

In Amergin's song (for he sang this, according to Lebor Gabála), the fertility of the land is seen as being linked with the fertility of the sea.

It is a curious consideration about the salmon's return to its birthplace that, in many instances, the fish will die there, after the spawning, if in fact it hasn't been snared by a predator on the way upstream. Salmon carcases are important nutrient sources for the river, and sometimes for the land in proximity to it too. But of course the primary recipient of the nourishment of the salmon is the human.

Nourishment of the mind must come before nourishment of the spirit. You are what you eat. No wonder, then, that the boy Fionn should have been imbued with all the wisdom and indeed the *imbas* when he innocuously consumed part of the salmon at Fiacc's Pool. To the poet, the salmon represented enrichment of the body, the mind and the soul. I have long found it interesting, in this regard, that the hazelnut is a highly nutritious food. It has been in our diet in the Boyne Valley since the first people arrived here after the ice melted.

There is no evidence, of course, to suggest that salmon eat hazelnuts, but in the poetic world view, possibilities are imagined, not dismissed. It is likely that the very notion of fish eating nuts that drop from a sacred tree has a poetic implication that cannot be easily extrapolated and summarised in the ordinary waking-hours rational language of humans.

At Inber Colpa, with his harbour song, Amergin Glúngeal summoned the salmon to arrive in a huge outburst, an ejaculation. There is mating symbolism here too. The thronging eruption of fish, swimming through the birth canal, are all seeking that holy birth-egg, the Segais ovum of their first spawning. How many would make it, and how many would die trying?

What does the cormorant say?

From that same bedroom window, in the house of my youth, I used to watch the floating cormorant on the Boyne. He would disappear into the water, leaving only those growing rings that you see when you throw a stone into the river. A minute later, he would surface again nearby. What is it that you see down there, cormorant, beyond the swimming things that would satiate your hungry belly?

When you go down there, do you tempt yourself with a feast greater than you can manage? Would you wish more for a salmon than a smolt between your beak? Is it a fair fight — salmon versus cormorant? Who would come away more scathed, from the battle for a larger meal? Remembering your tussles with the salmon, perhaps you've opted for smaller fry.

Did you talk to the salmon, in that minute when I saw you disappear, that minute when you became a bird out of air, a feathered, winged fish of the water? What did you say to him, beneath the gentle swells of Bóinn's watery skin? Did you ask him about his journey? Did you ask him where he came from, and where he is going?

Perhaps, as you conversed, he told you of his many wanderings in the great seas and oceans of the wide world. Did he tell you of his dark beginnings in the pool of ignorance? Did he tell you of the magic nuts, and his coming to knowledge? Did he tell you of his great awakening, at the coming of the one who would walk against the sun so that he could be set free?

Did he tell you of the eruption, and the sad breaking of the woman?

Did he tell you of his coming to the ford at Trim, and the floodgate at Slane, and the pool of Fiacc beneath Brú na Bóinne?

Did he tell you of his first taste of salt water, where salt entered the wounds at Inber Colpa?

Passing there, from Boyne to sea, there was a great sadness for the salmon. He was leaving the land of Ériu, the land of Bóinn, and the unknown waters of a great journey lay ahead of him. Perhaps he knew, though, something of that call to return. Even then, as a young fish encountering the sea for the first time, he sensed that, in the last days, there would be a coming back — a return from which there would be no return.

There was a calling now, from the sea, a great voice which beckoned him to wild adventures in boundless waters under many suns and moons and stars. The creature who had been so limited in the confines of the well of Segais would become lost in the vastness of his own self-exploration. He would go where it was bright and dark. He would swim in the shallows and the depths. He would go where he would be lonely, and where the ocean teems with life. He would encounter many creatures in the fabulous ocean, and would find many adventures in the flowing current of his life's exciting moments.

But for all that, he would remember, even faintly, that there would come a calling to return; a hearkening to the sounds of Segais, the sounds of the spawning pools where life began and where it would end.

He didn't think about it too much, perhaps, for when the cormorant spoke, he told the salmon he would see him again, on his way back up the river, on his final journey.

'It will be easy for you to forget,' said the cormorant, 'the sound of the *cnó* plopping into the water above you, when you are far removed from Segais in the deep waters of the world. For a while — a long while — you will know freedom; boundless freedom. The ocean will lull you to forgetfulness, and in the passing of the months and years you will grow to a mighty size. But the *cnó* spots on your back, which are hidden from you, will be like a mystery burden that you will carry — a mystery that will call you to return to the fresh water one last time.'

And I wonder now, all these years later, if the surfacing cormorant was the one who initiated the salmon, so that the salmon would have some knowledge of its future return.

Swimming on, from the Bridge at the Ford, and beneath the great span of the Boyne Viaduct out along the estuary, past Mornington and the Maiden's Tower, and out to the Bar, I wonder if the salmon had taken one last look at the broken goddess in the water, and the monster's bones, and thought about a homecoming. Far in the future, maybe, he would pass here once again.

The salmon was too big to eat, but I like to think that the cormorant had given him a good bite.

'Keep a listen,' the cormorant might have said.

'Keep a listen for that distant song that calls you to your deeper self, that voice within that beckons you to the submerged worlds of your abyssal wanderings.'

The salmon might not have understood at the time, but the proper time for remembering would come.

'Most importantly, remember to listen for that familiar voice, the voice of the salmon in the pool. Hearken to the sound, little fish, of a new song being sung on the shore of the Boyne at Inber Colpa. You will not know when or where you will hear it, and you might be far off in the great vastness of the western ocean, but the song will come to you, even when you least expect it.'

'What song?' the salmon asked.

'The song of Amergin.'

And the memory would come back to him then, of the place in the Boyne where the tide turns, where the fresh water meets the salty, and where wild adventures in the world begin and end. The warrior at the ford, and the poet by the pool, and the fisherman at the weir, will all remember the smolt, the initiate of the ocean. And the writer at the Bridge over the Ford, who saw you off as you swam towards the sea at Inber Colpa, will be there to greet you on your return.

171

A Meeting at the Ford

There will be sweet music, and a great song, on the day of your homecoming, and although it will be tinged with sadness, your passion for Segais, your desire for source, will overcome all. You left as a child, but will return as a man.

Listen. Listen for the voice.

Hearken. Hearken to the birth of song.

The one who comes to Inber Colpa as a salmon in a pool will be the one to herald your return. The one who is a wind on the sea will sing for your homecoming. He will be an ocean wave and a roar of the sea; a powerful ox; a hawk on a cliff; a dewdrop in sunshine; a boar for valour. But most importantly:

A salmon in the pool.
A salmon in the pool.
A salmon in the pool.

What land is better than this island of the setting sun? What better place to die, than the spawning pools of your first imaginations? As I look down from the bridge, perhaps I will see deep down a sky full of stars, and a new world, and my heart will know gladness.

In the quickening twilight, I might catch a glimpse of something, down there in the depths of blue. A flickering light, perhaps? A light from an old world.

The old well is still in you, although you have wandered far from the pools of your first emergence.

Listen. Listen for the voice.

Although silently you might vie against the current of your own life, you might in the dimness of the water perceive that golden hue of love-light in the evening twilight. Swimming ever onwards, your silvery scales flickering in the way, you might wonder how it was that spawn became smolt, and smolt became the great salmon of the deep ocean.

It all happened so fast, and the days glimmered overhead, oscillating from day to night and from night to day again. The greatest of your concerns was the one that you pushed to the back of your mind. That day, when emboldened smolt raced for the sea at Drogheda, the cormorant said he would see you again. There would be a bittersweet return.

Did you imagine it would come so soon?

The race of your ocean days now over, there is just one race left to run — the run to Segais.

Leaving Inber Colpa back then, as you first breathed the salty water, and knowing that you would have to seek to return, how would you find your way back to the gleaming Boyne?

And when I think about that, something in me recognises the astronomer in you. The navigator. The surveyor. With all that we have done and achieved, as humans, speaking to each other across the world

173

through thin air and sending men and women into space, I feel hopelessly inadequate as a creature of the wild world in the presence of one who is able to find Linn Fiacc and Segais having wandered out into the deep oceans of the world.

I bow to you, O holy salmon, at the bridge over the ford as you make your final return to the pools where you were first spawned. You must, like me, have eyes turned towards heaven, for the one who loves the stars and is at home with the night will never feel lost in the wide world.

Coming back now, at the place where the tide turns near the old ford, I will tip my hat, and shed a tear, for a dear old friend who is making his last journey under the sky of stars.

Standing at the bridge, I might wonder which of the stars has guided you home. In your sea of water, was there a sea of stars? In the deepest pools of your journeying, have you seen starlight?

What is visible down there, in the darkness, for a salmon with an eye for the heavens? When you ascended out of Segais, what was the first star that you saw? When you descended for your first great embarkation to the deep waters of the Atlantic, what was the last star you saw before you took the plunge?

What, in your Piscean nature, called you to the shore of the sea of stars and called you 'astronomer'?

Did you see yourself reflected in the great river of the sky?

From pool to ocean the smolt went, a tiny, sparkling light in a vast ocean of shining things. What single flickering light matters a jot among a scintillating array of stars whose light strives to us through the darkness for billions of miles?

Perhaps that faint and obscure star was the one that guided you home — the one that we ignored because we were chasing grand patterns in the sky. I saw two fish swimming, out of water. Two fish of the air. But you just saw stars — the stars of your better nature.

Was it a less familiar form that called you to begin the journey home?

Hearing a birth of song, did you perceive the poet-warrior, standing with his foot, his bright-kneed leg, on the shore of Eridanus?

You heard his voice, as a wind on the sea out in the distant waters of your magnificent ocean.

As a wave of the ocean, he lapped over you then, as you watched Orion dip his toes in the sea.

And he roared. He roared in such a way that you've never heard the ocean roar, and it shook you and stirred you and called you to remember the cormorant at Drogheda, and the heron by the shore at Oldbridge, and the angler at Slane, and the otter by the weir. The song of Amergin called for a dance — a dance of delice. The dance of delight.

Am goeth I muir	I am a wind on the sea
Am tonn trethain	I am a wave of the ocean
Am fuaim mara	I am a roar of the sea

The birth of song was a powerful ox for you, crossing the river at the ancient ford, his herdsmen ushering him to the summer booley and fresh pastures.

The birth of song was a hawk on a cliff, an ancient voice of the wild, the one that told in sacred story the adventures of the restless creature called man, the restless creature called salmon.

In all our migrations, the hawk in us calls us to remember home. Our nest, her bosom. Bring us home, mother.

Full of knowledge, you are returning to the place where your thirst for knowledge began. The boar, brave for the rut, eats the mast from the forest floor and readies itself for the next confrontation.

The salmon in the pool eats the sacred *cnó* and finds itself hungry; hungry for the ocean.

The meagre pool is transformed. It becomes a lake on a plain, and all the water that streams from it seeks the ocean. Seeing the possibility of an ocean life for itself, the smolt dreams of those eager waterways, the ones that lead from innocence in the shade of the hazel grove to a life of enlightenment in the open sea.

THE WAY OF THE WHITE COW

Only one thing will lead it back, a calling to the hearth where once the fry were given an impossible task — go to the ocean, live your life, and come back again in the end.

One thing. That voice from the ancient world. The sweetest of songs. A chiming bell. A gong crash. The birth of song at the shore of the Boyne. And all the leagues that separate you from your homeland, your birthing pools, are as a meagre hop for the song thrush, leaping from one bush to the next. Like you, the thrush is speckled. Like you, the constellations are imprinted upon it. No creature with an eye for the stars will ever lose sight of home.

I imagine that it was great Orion, setting his bright foot on the surface of the ocean as he went down in the west, that first reminded you of the sacred pool from which Bóinn became ocean. Somewhere way out in the west, far beyond the coasts of the sacred island where the goddess is still venerated, far beyond the reach of a human voice amid the relentless noise of the crashing waves, you heard it. You heard the song of Amergin as Orion stepped into the sea.

Who will bring the fish from the house of the sea but he? Who will summon the *cassar find,* the bright hail, from the river's shore or the mountain tops, but he?

177

Whose voice will be heard, far beyond where others can reach, except his?

In the late part of the day, you have heard that call.

In the blue hour of evening, when the ocean has swallowed the sun and the oranges and azure hues fade to a deepening black, you turn swiftly and defiantly for the final journey.

The harbour song calls for a white flash and an eruption of fish.

Íascach muir! Íascach muir!
A fishful sea! A fishful sea!

Knowing that you are fading, as the blue hour dips to starless black, you turn for home.

The Boyne calls.

Bóinn calls.

Ériu calls.

Amergin calls.

The sea can only remain fishful if there is another spawning. You must go back.

On the first night of your journey home, I imagine that you watched carefully the Milky Way, that great river of stars painted onto the ceiling of the domed night. The Way of the White Cow. The river of the broken goddess. The river of the dismembered monster. The river of the silvery salmon. Remember, nothing dies; there is only a return.

And Uisneach will rejoice at your return.

And Tara will rejoice at your return.

And Síd in Broga will rejoice at your return.

At Sídh Nechtain, on the hill above Carbury village, a lamp-light flickers in the evening twilight. Three cup-bearers approach the king's private quarters. He demands to know why they have come at this late hour.

'We have heard a voice, a song,' they say. 'And the salmon is coming back.'

'Coming back where?' the king asks.

'The salmon wishes to return to Segais.'

'Quickly,' the king exclaims. 'We must make haste to the sacred well.'

At Tara, three servants approach the king.

'Why thy late coming?' he asks.

'Dear king,' they reply, 'we have heard a voice from the northeast, from Inber Colpa.'

'What does it say?'

'It is a voice that sings a new song. It is a voice that sings of a wind on the sea and an ocean wave. It is a voice that calls the fish from their house in the sea.'

The voice comes to them again, out of the northeast, so that the king hears it too. Turning around at Tara, looking in the opposite direction, they see the great warrior-poet constellation putting his foot on a hill in the southwest.

'What hill is that?' asks the king.

'Sídh Nechtain, of course,' they reply.

'It is happening,' says the king.

There is a white flash at Inber Colpa. The lapdog barks from the river bank and the curlew cries from the Maiden's Tower. There is an eruption, a burst of fish. The cormorant greets his old friend in the shadow of the arches in Drogheda.

'I told you I would see you again. You heard the song. Welcome back, son of the river, son of the sea.'

At the Bridge over the Ford, the astronomer who saw the meteor shower streaking through the Milky Way considered it a sign and stood waiting for the *cassar find*.

Smolt grown to salmon has come back to the place where the tide turns for one last race against Bóinn's relentless current. Watching for his old friend, he weeps for the poignant return. A teardrop falls from his cheek into the river, in the salmon's path. It will be the last salt water the fish encounters.

A New Song

An end is coming. And also a beginning. The salmon will expend all its energy and its life force in the heave to reach the spawning pool.

There's no making sense of it. The journeys of life are undertaken through necessity tinged with wanderlust. Limited by the tight confines of Segais, you were called to a great adventure. Your return is, in equal measure, sad and joyous. Perhaps in the future I will stand on the Bridge at the Ford and wait for the smolts and grilse, the offspring of your final act in the upper reaches of the Boyne. And a new race will begin.

For now, I am left to ponder the mystery of it all, and to wonder about all those things that lead one to great adventures. For now, my heart is full of heaviness. The smolt has come home to die. Resting in the pool at Linn Fiacc, at Rosnaree, I wonder if you will see the boy Fionn and the old man Finegas, at the shore, bowing to you as you pass. Will you see Elcmar at Síd in Broga, with his fork of white hazel? Will you pass the angler at the weir in Slane? At Ardmulchan there will be a swan-song. At Dunmoe, a setting moon. At Athlumney, a call of the buzzard and at Trim the bellowing of a bull. There will be a symphony for your return.

I never knew what *cassar find* was until that day — the day of your return.

At Inber Colpa, I watched and waited for you. I saw the boat of Amergin, the ship of the poet, passing the Bar. It carried a new song, a song for the awakening of many things that were, *cnó*-like, in darkness but awaiting a fabulous sundering and a reaching for the sky.

And as I waited on the river bank at Mornington, I heard and saw magnificent things.

The curlew called. He called me. He called you. And my heart was glad because the call of the curlew keeps us alive to our transcendent potentialities. If the curlew dies, we all die.

Flights of cormorants skimmed the water, and here and there they perched on the ancient beacons. They were the torchlights, leading you home.

There was a *cassar find* — a white hail — in the water and in the sky. A thousand salmon swam past, and a thousand trout, and a thousand eels.

Countless hundreds of birds swarmed in the air over Mornington village.

At the Maiden's Tower, there was a great glimmering. The water shimmered in huge undulations of silver and gold. A flock of geese, V-shaped, passed overhead, pointing the way home. And all the vessels of the world were offshore, or so it seemed, harvesting the fishful, fishful sea. The dark moon would break to dawning crescent, a sign for you, hanging in the evening air.

I saw you at Inber Colpa.

I saw you at the Bridge over the Ford.

I saw you at Brú na Bóinne.

I saw you at Linn Féic.

And as I looked, I saw something deep within myself. I saw a wild adventurer, ready to allow the well of my own soul to burst forth, opening to oceans of possibility.

I would hook no fish at the weir at Slane.

I would only want you to swim, and run, and fly, back to the place where your first *cnó* cracked open a magnificent awakening in you.

Fly now, O holy salmon.

Fly now, my little friend.

Fly on, to the place of your resting, to the beginning and the end.

Against all the odds, you have returned.

The fry of the pool, the smolt of the streamlet, the salmon of the deep world and the deeper heart, has come back to the source.

My own song has been born. I will sing a new song for you, dear friend, on your return to Segais.

The end (and the beginning)

GLOSSARY

Ail na Mireann: The Stone of Divisions at Uisneach. Also Umbilicus Hiberniae, the Navel of Ireland.

Amergin: Bard and spiritual leader of the Milesians, who came to Ireland to take it from the Tuatha Dé Danann. His epithet is Glúngeal, meaning 'bright knee'. He was the first of the Milesians to come ashore at Inber Colpa after calming the storm raised by the Tuatha Dé Danann to prevent the Milesian arrival. His name possibly derives from *Amhair-ghin*, meaning 'birth of song'.

Athair: Father.

Áth Cliath: The Ford of the Hurdles, an old name for Dublin in the Dindshenchas.

Áth Troim: The Ford of the Liver, an old name for the town of Trim, on the Boyne in County Meath.

Banba: One of a triad of guardian goddesses of Ireland along with Ériu and Fódla.

Battle of Moytura: Cath Maige Tuired was the great battle between the Tuatha Dé Danann and their mortal enemies, the Fomorians.

Bealtaine: Ancient festival of May, marking the beginning of summer.

Bóinn: The eponymous goddess of the river Boyne. Bóinn (also spelt Bóann) is from *Bó* meaning cow and *Finn* meaning bright.

Bradán Feasa: Irish name for the Salmon of Knowledge.

Brú na Bóinne: Irish name for the great megalithic monument complex of the Bend of the Boyne, incorporating Newgrange (Síd in Broga), Knowth, Dowth and many other monuments. Also spelt Brug na Bóinne.

Cailleach: A very ancient deity or otherworldly woman, often depicted as an old woman or hag.

Cleitech: The mound or *sídhe* to which Elcmar went after he was banished from Síd in Broga. Believed to have been located at Rosnaree, on the southern bank of the Boyne.

Cnó: Irish word for a hazelnut.

Cnoc: Hill or mound.

185

Cnogba: Old Irish name for Knowth monument at Brú na Bóinne. In one tale, it is said to derive from *cnó-guba*, the 'nut lament' from a mysterious ritual carried out there by Oengus Óg.

Conmaicne Rein: A mountain in the west (Connacht) upon which the Tuatha Dé Danann were said to have burnt their ships after arriving into Ireland. They did so in order that they would not retreat from their Fomorian enemies.

Cruachan Aí: Another name for the monument complex and royal centre at Rathcroghan, in the west of Ireland.

Dagda: Chief of the Tuatha Dé Danann, and builder and owner of Síd in Broga (Newgrange). He was a solar deity who lay with Bóinn to conceive the child Oengus Óg. He was the one who, according to Tochmarc Emire (The Wooing of Emer), killed the great monster (Mata). One of his possessions was a great cauldron, which was inexhaustible.

Danu: Mother of the gods, the Tuatha Dé Danann.

Dian Cécht: Healer god of the Tuatha Dé Danann.

Dindshenchas: A medieval collection of myths about sacred or eminent places in Ireland.

Donn Cuailnge: The great 'Brown Bull of Cooley' from the Táin epic. Its great rival was Finnbennach (see below).

Dubh Linn: The ' Black Pool'. An old name for Dublin city.

Eber: First joint Milesian king of Ireland with his brother, Erimón. These two were brothers of Amergin.

Eithne: Another name for Bóinn. Also the name of Lugh Samildánach's mother.

Elcmar: A Tuatha Dé Danann deity who, in some threads of myth, was the owner of Síd in Broga/ Newgrange. Husband of Bóinn.

Erimón: First joint Milesian king of Ireland with his brother, Eber. These two were brothers of Amergin.

Ériu: Also spelt Éire, she was one of a triune of tutelary or guardian goddesses of Ireland when the Milesians arrived. Ireland (Éire-land) is named from her. The other two were Banba and Fódla.

Féth Fiada: Magical veil or mist of invisibility made for the Tuatha Dé Danann by Manannán. It had the ability to conceal them so that they were invisible to mortal eyes, or else they took on animal forms.

Finegas: Also known as Finegas the Wise. A druid who caught the Salmon of Knowledge at Linn Féic. But it was the youth Fionn Mac Cumhaill who consumed the fish's knowledge.

Finnbennach: The "white-horned". A great bull of the Táin Bó Cuailnge epic.

Finnflescach: The 'Bright and Flourishing Spring' or well of Uisneach. Also known as Tobernaslath.

Fintan: Full name Fintan Mac Bóchra, Fintan son of the Sea, he was the sole survivor of the early great flood, having come to Ireland with Cessair, a granddaughter of Noah. Fintan is also a name given to the Salmon of Knowledge in some myths.

Fionn Mac Cumhaill: Hero of the Fianna, a warrior band from medieval stories common in Ireland and in Scotland. His name might mean 'starry son of the hazel'. He was the one who received all the wisdom of the Salmon of Knowledge when he burnt his thumb on the fish at Linn Féic.

Fódla: One of a triune of tutelary goddesses of Ireland along with Banba and Ériu. (Also spelt Fótla).

Fulacht Fiadh: A prehistoric cooking pit or burnt mound.

Grá: Love.

Imbas: 'great knowledge'; foreknowledge; inspiration.

Inber Colpa: The estuary of the Boyne river. (Inber is pronounced Inver).

Lebor Gabála: The so-called Book of Invasions. Lebor Gabála Érenn (the Book of the Takings of Ireland) is a medieval manuscript containing mythic and pseudo-historical accounts of various invasions of or arrivals into Ireland in prehistory.

Lecc Benn: A stone mentioned in the Dindshenchas as being located on or near Newgrange/Síd in Broga. It is the stone upon which the great monster the Mata was said to have been killed.

Lia Fáil: Stone of Destiny at the Hill of Tara. The traditions of the stone suggest that it screamed aloud when the rightful king stood on it or placed his foot against it.

Linn Féic: Also Linn Fiacc. Fiacc's Pool, a mythical pool in the Boyne River close to Rosnaree where Finegas the Wise, a druid, is said to have caught the Salmon of Knowledge. However, the young boy Fionn Mac Cumhaill burnt his thumb cooking the fish and when he sucked it to cool it, he gained all the wisdom of the Salmon of Knowledge.

Lough Derravaragh: A swan-shaped lake in County Westmeath.

Lugh: One of the greatest of the Tuatha Dé Danann deities, variously known as Lugh Samildánach (the many-gifted), Lugh mac Ethnenn (son of Eithne) and Lugh Lámhfada (Lugh of the Long Arm). Pronounced "lou" or "loo".

Magh Mell: 'Pleasant Plain', an Irish otherworld or fairyland.

Manannán: Also known as Manannán Mac Lir, he was the sea deity of the Tuatha Dé Danann.

Mata: A great monster of mythology, said to have been slain at Lecc Benn at Brú na Bóinne and dismembered, its body thrown piece by piece into the Boyne. Its shin-bone was said to have formed the Boyne Estuary. (Variant spelling Mátha, Matae).

Máthair: Mother.

Muirthemne: The plain covered by the sea. Muirthemne covers the area mostly known as County Louth today, but also included Brú na Bóinne, where Dagda, having killed the great monster Mata, succeeded in making the sea waters recede from the land.

Oengus Óg: The son of an illicit union between the sun god Dagda and Bóinn, he later became owner of Síd in Broga (Newgrange), which he won from the Dagda by trickery. His name is associated with youth, and it was said of him 'young is the son who was conceived in the morning and born between that and the evening of the same day'.

Oillphéist: A great water snake or river dragon/serpent of Irish folklore.

Oisín: Warrior and poet of the Fianna and son of Fionn Mac Cumhaill.

Rí: Irish word for king.

Rockabill: Two small islands off the east coast, visible from the Boyne Estuary.

Rosnaree: A location just southwest of the Boyne with views across Brú na Bóinne to Knowth and Newgrange. Said to have been the location of Linn Féic and Cleitech.

Samhain: An old festival date coinciding with modern Hallowe'en, marking the beginning of winter.

Segais: The mythical well from which the Boyne River was said to have sprung.

Sétanta: Boyhood name of the great warrior of Táin Bó Cuailnge, Cúchulainn. He was said to have been conceived at Síd in Broga/Newgrange by Lugh and Deichtine.

Síd in Broga: The old Irish name for the great monument of Newgrange at Brú na Bóinne. Rendered as Sídhe an Bhrú in modern Irish.

Sídh Nechtain: The otherworldly residence of Nechtain, said to have been located close to the Well of Segais, which was also called Nechtain's Well.

Sídhe: An old Irish name for some of the monuments, including Síd in Broga (Newgrange). Its meaning is not exactly known, but is usually translated as 'fairy mound' or 'otherworld mound'. The implication is that *sídhe* represents a portal or opening into other worlds or realms. Pronounced 'shee'.

Tathlum: An ancient weapon used by the deity Lugh in the battle against the Fomorians. It was a giant ball said to have been formed of the brains of the enemies hardened with lime.

Tea: Wife of Erimón, first Milesian king of Ireland, who chose Druim Caín (Hill of Tara) as the place from which they would reign. The Dindshenchas suggests Tara was Temair, from Tea-Mur, the Wall or Rampart of Tea.

The Bar: The colloquial name for a shifting bank of sand at the mouth of the Boyne, over which vessels must cross before entering the river.

Tobernaslath: The 'Bright and Flourishing Spring' or well of Uisneach. Also known as Finnflescach.

Tuatha Dé Danann: Early deities, some of them associated in mythology with the building of the great monuments of Brú na Bóinne.

Uisneach: A hill containing many monuments, including some from the Neolithic, located in modern day Westmeath. It was the sacred and mythic centre of Ireland, location of Ail na Mireann, the Stone of Divisions. Associated with the death of Lugh and also the place where Amergin negotiated with Ériu about the future naming of Ireland.

SOURCES

vii. Campbell, Joseph (1988) [1949], *The Hero With a Thousand Faces,* Paladin Grafton Books, p. 3.

P. 81. 'Only the wounded physician heals.' From Jung, C. G. (1974) [1963], *Memories, Dreams, Reflections,* The Fontana Library, p. 155.

P.111. See *Tales of the Elders of Ireland:* A new translation of Acallam na Senórach by Ann Dooley and Harry Roe, Oxford World's Classics, Oxford University Press, 2008 [1999].

P. 165. '*Íascach muir!* A Fishful sea!', etc. R.A. Stewart Macalister (ed.), *Lebor Gabála Erenn, The Book of the Taking of Ireland,* Part V (1956), Irish Texts Society, pp. 114-115.

P. 176. '*Am goeth I muir,* I am a wind on the sea', etc. Ibid, pp. 110-111.